Riding this mad thunder bolt roller coaster, always take a deep breath then plunging into the unknown. You have no choice really; you've showed up, paid your admission and are in it for the ride. Jumping off, bailing now would be suicide for sure. Besides the cork is off the bottle, the glasses are being raised and there's not a plastic monkey in the house. These are your people, your kind, sophisticated agents of hysteria! Full throttle line jumping fools.

Blinded by the array of experience that's oozing out as if it were a remote mountain spring. Take heed not to slow down, this will bring absolute death, I've seen it! In a mosaic blur you watch them slow down, reach out their arm and crumble back into the soulless shuffle of empty existence.

Embrace disaster as if it were a road-map to your psyche. The jackals will circle your rotting carcass, but the radar picks up on the howls and sends out the institution, puts leaches to you, slice and dice and re-wire your hard drive. After this is done they wind up your dial to release the awkward remains of a defeated soldier. "Don't go out the way" I say to myself...

Where the fuck am I? I don't recognize any of this. Great mother of God, this is it! I've been swallowed up by the fucking beast! I'm in the under-belly. They must have drugged me and shoved me in easily as I was off balanced with weak knees. This fucking monster will have to shit sometime and I'll be dislodged from its bowels.

The acid is starting to eat at me. I think I'll be all right soon..?. Trudge through this vermin darkness, if it looks as bad as it smells I don't want to see it anyhow. Amazing a van! It's incomprehensible the insatiable appetite this beast has, IT'S A FUCKING PIG for Christ sakes! Holy fuck they're onto me! I've been raving out loud to myself, it may be too late. Never just fucking die, AHHHHHHHHH keys! Ignition and throttle! I could hear the beast cry horribly as I stomped the throttle to where it belongs, ON THE FLOOR! In low gear, there's second, and third! The piercing screams of the hounds…! Music, that will drown them out, take that fuckers! Now there it is, New Orleans. At the last turn I lost them!

There needs to be a warning back there, it could take years to get out of that mess. It was so dark in there that even the stars are blinding, Ahh! Off the road, on the road, got to keep my focus. The alligators are just waiting for a fool like you. Man that was some acid. It looks like the northern lights. No it can't be, not this far south. Let's see, its 1:13 am, why sleep now?

I'm more like alcohol, booze, beer, liquor, LIQUOR! THAT'S IT! and how about an alligator hat, this is Louisiana! The town is restless and I can see already that I'm goanna like this. I've got to be methalodical about this, raise no suspicion. Easy enough, because like the voice on the radio just said, "This is the big easy!" I've found my parking spot to make into my central headquarters. A nice dark area just past Jackson Square in the heart of the French Quarters, that runs parallel with the Mississippi river, with parking until 11am.

Now all I have to do is stay calm until I drench myself in liquor. I think I'll run like the devil is chasing me to the state liquor store, slam a fifty down on the counter, grab a bottle of rum and start chugging it while I make my way to the cooler, reach in, grab a can of coke and wrap my drawling mouth around it!

Perfect, nobody gets hurt. From there I will make my connections…

MMM-Oh Yeah; Why not, a pair of these springy eye glasses, 5 packs of Marlboros, 2 bic lighters and an alligator hat. 'WHAT NO ALLIGATOR HAT!!?! I THOUGHT I WAS DEALING WITH A LEGITIMATE BUSINESS."

I like it, a mission. "Well this'll work for starters; the gator hat will be taken care of soon enough. 62.35, here you go, keep the change and throw two more cans of coke on there, this is a big BOTTLE of RUM! Thank you then."

Let's see, my friends will have to wait. I've got to find an alligator hat…

The crashing sound interrupted my train of thought. Maybe these glasses aren't such a good idea inside of the store. Nonsense, they're perfectly reasonable, nothing broke. A harmless mistake, I walked into a pyramid display of two liter coke bottles.

"Here, I'll start by grabbing these ones and helping re-stack them." I say

Just then the clerk becomes hostile. I grip my pack and slowly start stepping backwards. No sudden moves, slow. Hitting the door I break for it! Ungrateful bastard this probably happens every other day.

"Hello there, Hello to you, Happy Gradi Mas to you too." Fascinating, one minute I was stuck on the desolate highways cutting through no-where Middle America and now this! The epicenter of a counter culture freak-for-all, take no prisoners Mardi Gras!

I'm friends with the streets and with those who walk upon them. I'm in the "industry." The code word for the back-bone of workers that work to make New Orleans what it is for the millions of visitors. What this means is at bars like the 'Decatur' you get half off your drinks. The Decatur Bar is right across the street from the House of Blues and as you are sliding in and out of the backstage door of the "House of Blues' you can drink all week on what you would spend in just one night at the H.O.B. some establishments totally violate you when it comes to pricing their drinks and have no respect for you.

Now on with the freaks! Every bit of insanity one could ever wish for is here and seducing you into a part of you that stays dormant for most of your life. The hairy beast, the animal, the rooster is clawing in my chest until I'm a strange

combination of supernatural elements. Fire in my
fingertips and my spliced corrupted genes!

These God forsaken glasses have got to go!
Maybe they'll work when I'm not so fucked up.
The springs jump around and it looks like I'm
entering a vortex or their goanna pull my eyes
out! Past the piano bar, WOW- Back up, look at
the exquisite creature glowing who's laid out
across the piano and is singing. I get all the way

up next to her. This is it, I've met her. I've met her a thousand times! This one though, she's different, she's piercing my eyes with volcanic passion. I take this opportunity to obsessively drink some rum, fumbling I find the sugar wash. Opening it the can erupts, I jump backwards and it's all you hear. No more singing, no more piano, just fizzle like someone cracked open a fire hydrant, and then SMACK! The can hits the ground and Explodes open and sprays everybody like a cluster bomb within a ten foot radius. I had to be right next to the piano. So much for not drawing attention…

Sweat beads up immediately and the glaring eyeballs take my breath away! She does it, she laughs uncontrollably! The leader and the run down people at their table join in. I'm a gentleman, immediately I take off my shirt and start drying her off.

"My name is sky." She says through her laughter.

"I love sky, I'm Jasper. Would you like some rum to go with your coke?" I help her off the piano and as she slides off her body rubs along mine. I just about burst into a stiffy and while were close I do. She's all women, all 5'10" of her.

With a southern draw she tells me "Rum and coke are my favorite, thank you Jasper."

"I'm in love with you, I mean I love your voice." I say and she breaks into a giggle. This girl has passion, with eyes as white as a wolf's. I'm lost, paralyzed, I hear the tickle of the piano but it's nothing with-out her and I'm not letting go. "Would you like some rocket fuel?" I blurt out.

"Hell Yeah, I'm going to fucking like you!"

I stopped listening after the I'm going to fuck part and grabbed her hand and pulled her to a table in the back.

"No, the other way. I've been looking for a way to politely break away."

"I'm your man, I'm trained in this. I sensed your need, this was all planned. The stars are in our sky." Now to cover myself, this could get rude, I'm stealing their star. "Oh no, just getting fresh air to dry her off. We'll be right back in, cue us with moon dance."

"You're bad, this feels good though. I've been coming to Mardi Gras since I was five, but this is the first year I've come alone. I'm meeting up with friends when I get bored."

"Call me friend and never get bored again! Here, stick out your tongue." I give her the communion and steal a kiss. Mother can she kiss!

"Your strange, but in a good way. Alexis is my real name, but I prefer Sky. Sky is my hustler name."

"What so you sell?"

"Play-doh."

"In what flavors?"

"Blueberry and sin."

"Good enough, I like both! Where are you from?"

"Jackson Mississippi, well 25 miles out in the Bayou. I bake pies when I sleep."

I melted just then at the pies and had to kiss her talented ass. Our faces held together for what seems like forever as we pull kiss on each others lips, biting teasing one another. The moist air and humid New Orleans night welding our energy together in a cosmic fire. The kiss peaks me out and I am no longer human, I am a sphere of light energy. Its her turn, she'll have to hold us together. We found each other right on schedule. She wanted saved from the piano, I needed a kiss and here we are, thank you Lord! Out of control, but control isn't one of my favorite states, I prefer chaos! Women scare easy, I've cosmically lassoed this one in. It all seems innocent, but how long will it be before she breaks down? Freaks out, has to much and loses her grip?

Just then it turns into what looks like a bad movie. A whole block of them! Sweat Jesus, I don't want to have to hurt anybody. Panic strikes me, I'm outnumbered and even with my sidekick we wouldn't stand a chance in hell if these folks want to become friendly outside of their group. They're wearing leather pants with their asses cut out, carrying leather whips, a couple have dog collars on and have broke off their masters leash. Women and men looking for new pets. Almost through themand then E-GADS! I'm stopped in

my tracks, petrified I can't move! Sky tugs me,
but right flank closes in, left flank closes in.
Behind me I can the crunch of leather and the
smell of body odor mixed with leather, mixed
with a strange smell of ass permeates my nostril.

Before this gets nasty something has to be
done. I clench Sky's hand, reach inside my pack
and pull out my air horn.
EEEEEEERRRRRRRNNNNNN! The blast
scatters them enough for us to make a break
through. Break on through, break on through,
Yep-Yep-Yep-Alright!

Sky looks at me with elevated curiosity. I
reach around and grab her left breast, hold it. She
reaches down and grabs my balls. Fever breaks
out, my life is in her hands.

"Yes this is real. You and me may only have
one night, but with the fuel induced intensity of a
thousand relationships!" I say.

"I'm young, that's all I'm looking for." She says.

"How old are you?" I ask.

"22, in March I'll be 23."

"Holy shit! Pisces or Aries?"

"Pisces, my B-Day is on the 17th."

"I'm on the 24th, an Aries, Just after the cusp."

"How you handled that back there was something else, the look on the morphodites faces when you blasted them had me laughing! My ears are still ringing!." Sky says

Freaks are the law. I fall into 'free and easy wanderer mode, exposed to almost all species of humanity. Scientists have it wrong. Psychologists are close, but they don't continue the mind through the body. This is the human jungle, with rare and undiscovered forms of people. Some are nothing more than a virus, then there are others who take on the presence of a universe.

Both of us are lost in the muddied waters of our minds. As we are fumbling down the sidewalk through people the doors fly open to a store and on the walls are leather masks. I think of the alligator mask and yank Sky in for a look....

"Do you have any alligator hats!" I ask.

"What?" THE STORE CLERK ASKS as he is busy moving through the people in the store to come closer to me.

I repeat my question when he gets close to me. "Do you have any alligator hats?" And further explain the situation.

After thirty minutes and two hundred dollars later we emerge from the store with 2 devilish masks but no god damn alligator hats! My mask looks like it is on fire with red colors and black in the folds. The mischievous eyes consume the world and look like they are on fire. Sky's mask is pink with dark red highlights and looks like a leather pixie mask. The pink is a sexy compliment to her juicy lips. No alligator hats but he did give me a name. He gave me a lead of an old mojo man who makes a gator costume every couple of years and lives thirty minutes outside town. This old mojo man is rumored to make suits for people and may have some already made. He gave me a warning of going early because there are strange folk out round the bayou. Emmett is his name and he has a lazy eye, blind in this world and vision of the other world, and other folklore about him.

"Your Satan and I'm Satan's bitch!" Sky says.

"I don't know about the Satan part, but I definitely like the sound of you being my bitch!"

"I thought you would. I'm a good girl and I like your power of corruption over me." Sky says.

"Don't forget about the drive to use it!" I say.

I almost slipped into a repulsive puddle of puke. Some poor bastard wasted all that money on food and drinks only to lose them. Beads are everywhere you step and quick bare breasts are flashing like headlights on the L.A. freeway. Frenchman street is where the locals hang and there is no need for beads. On Frenchman Street the common dress is body paint, exotic costumes and lots of feathers mixed in with freakishly creative wardrobes. If your not in costume, they actually take offense there. I found out several lifetimes ago when I rudely joined the locals out of costume and was told "go get in costume or go away."

Noises of raging hand drums are echoing off the old buildings and mixing with primal screams and loud voices blending together. Here is where lust will pull a couple apart quicker than a space shuttle launch, especially without having a history. No worries. Fire spinners come into view and I lift my head back letting out a here I am, the Devil himself yell.

Delirious dope fiends chase and mingle. "One coke can left and a lotta rum! Nows the time Sky." I say.

"Who knew, this is the first time I've been down this far. Wait a minute, is that bar called the 'Dragon's Den?"

"Fuck yeah! Bean bags and low Chinese tables along with the best intimate personal in your face atmosphere you can find. Pot smoke billowing out the windows, along with inhibitions.

I've driven blindly drunk from there a many nights. Tonight I'm thinking 'sex on the terrace!" I say.

"I don't know how to tell you this, but your face is falling off!" Sky says.

"Well your eyes are so deep I'm probably lost in there, let me look. MMMmm my God, you're a fucking animal, the equivalent to me in female form! Lets get lost in these costumes."

She's fiery, I can see the glow of blue under her skin. So alive, hanging onto my breath. I know now we are inseparable and I'm glad. I'll have to take it easy on her, I want her to last, one drink for her and two for me!"

"The sex odyssey parade" is beginning to split the crowd. The king is Ernie-K-Doe, a 60's music legend. The first float is guys and girls dressed in tight white, carrying sperms on sticks all swimming around a giant vagina float. I lose it laughing! Sky and I share a lip smacking kiss and my body is stuck in her pulse. Her energy goes up and around and drives me into her glowing embrace. Her lips are trembling and she's making this sweet sound, looking at me confused and delighted.

"The acid has taken me through a thousand worlds, I see the diamonds of your soul exploding into mine." Sky says.

"Something I have to tell you. That wasn't real acid we ate, I was just fooling with you." I say to her as her eyes are going around like oceans swirling around her pupils as big as globes.

"SHUT-UP!" She says and smacks me, then reaches behind me head and gives me a huge kiss.

"There's sensory overload here; The sounds, the voices, the beautiful colorful costumes, the fire breathers, the drummers, and you!" I say.

My hellish ride doesn't even seem like it was real. I miss being on my own, trailing my imagination, but this is rare. Something about Sky, Alexis, her Mississippi and sin flavored play-doh that I Know I don't want to walk away from.

"How about we follow the parade?" Sky says.

"Yeah, now that's my kind of girl! Lets go!" I say. This is the week that doesn't exist and universal things can happen in the broken time voids. This is where the real life happens that makes you know you're doing something right for your soul and not just a pencil pusher.

The street widens and the cars begin to float and move back and forth organically pulsating. Sky runs her nails along my neck and down my arm. I try to speak, but at the moment I'm frantic, nervous, high, in AWE. Words sound like spinning bubbles. I'm experienced, I won't lose it. Something equivalent to a nuclear reactor is in my head, splitting reality instead of atoms. Sky must notice it too, her eyes are chasing the funnel. The visuals are great! We've lost the parade, I notice the streets are thinning out and were not far from central headquarters.

"Sky, lets hike it to my vehicle. We can hang there for a while, then I've got a place reserved we can spend the morning at while we regain ourselves."

"Huh? It's amazing this is the closest I've felt to someone and we've only met three hours ago!

Yes to your question, I'm ready to get off my feet and stretch out with you."

Running, her hair glistens with the street lights. The old buildings with their old world architecture give a feeling of being in a small town. We all out chase each other, running down the streets madly until my hand smacks the van.

"The blue midnight express, pile in, were going for a ride!" Make no mistake, we are truly fucked up, stumbling into the surreal toaster box with wheels.

"Wait, come back here with me first." Sky pulls me into the back of the van.

There isn't any resistance, resistance is futile, not to mention stupid! Our body heat soars, the intensity, the desire is so powerful! One look into her glowing silver eyes is like looking out over the peak of Mt. Everest. Her breast are round and velumpsous! Shredding the clothes off our bodies, neither of us are speaking we are nibbling and breathing heavily with the feeling of ecstasy boiling over our bodies. She laughs and her body jumps as I go down on her. She's completely shaved! After the greatest sex I've had in my life the sky is in early morning twilight and seagulls are filling the deep blue horizon. We hop into the front seats and breath in the kaleidoscope sky shifting glances from outside to each other.

"I feel really close to you, I haven't –WOW– All I can say is WOW!" Sky says.

"I wouldn't believe it if I weren't here." I say.

"Really, and it feels like its just starting. Hey the park next to the zoo by Tulane University has this giant Oak tree that is ancient." Sky says.

"I know exactly the one!" I blurt out, interrupting her. "Lets go, to the tree!"

"Feels more like a magic carpet ride than a
van. I see geometric shapes shifting like a Persian
rug everywhere I look." Sky says.

I enjoy the wholeness she brings. It grounds me from my absurdity. We shuttle sharing words, passing them back and forth the way a weaver would with one finishing the others sentence but they never end and we keep going round and round. Then my imagination slips beyond reason.

Make way! Don't have no brakes, THE GAS IS STUCK! Past one cop, past two. I feel like I'm the king of insanity. We'll just have to make it to the river, drive right in and then wait on the bank for the cops to leave. No sizeable loss, avoid capture at any price… Oh yes, green light. Almost there … just a bad vision, everything is operating fine but this intersection is funky???

"What's going on in there?" Sky looks at me wildly.

"Oh if you only knew, I'll take you there, but not this morning. My favorite time of the day, all five minutes of it is now, Sunrise exploding on the horizon. Here take a picture of me driving. You know you may have to keep me out of jail today." I say.

"Happy to oblige, thank you for sharing, I've been inspired."

At the river we stop for a view, this morning is high ripples of orange and yellow on the thin veil of clouds. Its around the bend, the Oak tree.

"Fucking awesome, no matter how many times I visit here I'm blown away." Sky says.

"Me too!"

The Oak tree is at least 10 feet wide and the first branch is about 30 feet off the ground and extends for what seems like forever out to touch the ground at least 70 feet away from it. You can walk right up this serpent branch holding onto another branch that's at head level to the center of the oak tree and be held by the ancient tree 30 feet above the ground. We aren't here alone, there's a chick burning sage and waving it around the tree. We go straight up it and fire up an early morning joint of some killer homegrown. The zoo fence isn't far off and we can see cheetah's laying down. The tree is awesome, its told this used to be a hanging tree back in the days of lynching.

Local kids sneak onto the Navy boats and steal the 4" thick heavy docking ropes and climb up the tree and tie them to swing on. There are two ropes tied way up in the tree top about 70 foot up and about 40 foot away from each other. You can swing on them, shimmy down like a fire pole and if you have brass balls you can swing off one of the branches and grab another rope in mid-air about 40 feet off the ground and starring death in the face. On the mirror of mortality you will be looking death in the face and it is your face! The reaper would be happy to take your soul after dropping from this height. I climb up and swing out from one of the branches to the other rope after an all night Tipitina's show. You will read that later...

Sage girl leaves and Chloe and I make love up in our perch safely out of view in the trees cradle. We balance out the evil that's been done here with carnal sex. My back got cut up from the bark and my blood becomes on with the ancient tree. Flutes play off in the distance like a mystical mountain misty haze and I would recommend putting in Codona Mumakata and eating a hit of acid at this point and come back to the book when your mind clears! Good God almighty, sweet Jesus, hall-a-lou-yah! You know what I am talking about?

We slide down one of the ropes back to terra firma. Man, the day is looking nice, that's all I need is some sunshine and colors in the breeze. Its Saturday, or is it Sunday? Neither of us are sure. At any rate southern hospitality is unlike no other, especially extended to a friend. My landlady may be home but hopefully she's gone for the weekend and we'll be gone before she returns or back to ourselves at least.

"Everything seems normal now except when I breathe the world pulls toward me and extends when I exhale." Sky says.

"I can't imagine being here at this moment with anybody else. Pick up the wagons Gertrude and wipe away that gravy from your lip, the high tide is up and we've got sea's to sail." I tell Sky.

"I fly a space ship, across the universe divide and when I reach the other side." Sky's singing and I join in… "When I reach the other side I'll find a place to rest my spirit if I can, perhaps I may become a highway man again, or I may simply be a single drop of rain, but I will remain and I'll be back again and again." We both sing together the song from the Highwaymen's first album, their song titled highwayman written by Jimmy Webb.

"That's one of my favorite songs! I can't believe that you know that one." I say.

"Remember Jasper, I am a southern girl and nothing says southern like the Highwaymen with Willie Nelson, Kris Kristofferson, Waylon Jennings and Johnny Cash!" Sky says.

"This is a space ship, you know." I say as I pound on the dashboard of the van.

"Oh-I bet, things seem pretty spacey!" Sky says.

Eyes are popping out all over the place as we are creeping down the road. I can't make out what half these people are. Smeared characters along Magazine street are only missing the circus music with a monkey organ grinder. They look like the heat shimmer on a hot highway, always on the horizon and dissolving into the air as we approach. I visualize stilt walkers, midgets, and elephants of my imagination all turn into ether on

me but somehow I sneak up on a group of them...
All of them are aware something unusual is going
to happen but how strange it is I don't think they
are prepared for. "Silver in the morning is just
right... Get in! Pile in the back. Time to get your
mind powered by rocket fuel!" I say, confirming
their curiosity. They receive their communion
and I drop them off in the French Quarter. They
toss me $70.00 thanking me for the wormhole I
have opened up for them! Dubiously smiling, I
drive off and tip my hat to them on their journey.

Marking the beginning of an unusual adventure
that knows not a beginning or an end but is dizzy,
our next stop is Vans Flying Burrito. Vans is
home to football sized burritos of your creation in
any combination. Great beers and the walls are
covered in abstract art done by the local artists
with art that drips surrealistically from the ceiling
to the floor.

Sky is fumbling around in the back and speaking in tongues. I yell 'HOLD ON! Then whip a 180 to get us to Wan's… Straight lines, draw no attention doesn't work. I like to throw off trailers by driving erratically, fast corners, wrong turn signals and run red lights! Throwing dust in the eyes, jamming radars, or a simple turn of the head make the difference between life or incarceration! There is a true art to my debauchery learned from years of abusing vehicles and countless court appearances. My favorite is wrong way down a one way street and you have to take the right-of-way, or else you get into an accident. I'm to far embedded in this counter culture to walk away from my faith in a higher guardian that watches over me, my angel of chaos who protects me with angel wings. You know what you are and why half it? The weak are easy prey, be the hunter, search out your enemies and breath in their face, make them hide. We don't need them anyhow.

"Ah- here it is! Pull yourself together, its burritos and beers!" I say.

The flyen burrito has an eclectic crew of servers assembled from artists to anarchists, tattooed and pierced, a true tribe of freaks. They don't leave you hanging on food orders either, if you ask for it they give you twice what you'd expect. Don't piss them off and chase them around or you'll be chased right the fuck out the door.

I feel strange because it has been 48 hours since I've slept or ate give or take 10 hours! This run is far from my record but with sleep deprivation and heavy alcohol intake time seems like eternity in sleep deprived states. As I walk in each footstep is an earthquake and everyone looks at us with their mouths chewing with eternity between every breath I take. Somehow a waitress notices my distress and leads us to the very back of the restaurant by the restrooms and in a smoking area. Its everything we need, speaking only four words to her "two pale ales please" my waitress disappears.

I could spend days melting here. I've already forgot about any and everything that was once on my mind. I think I'll smoke two cigarettes. One for me and one for my criminally insane side, my doppelganger. Sky is lost in some weird world all of her own. Oh God! What have I gotten myself into? Will she mother my children with some other fool off in Mississippi who believes he is the father? Or will I be on trial in ten years and get grilled by the prosecutor and then worse yet the anal ream by some evangelical judge who has no mercy for me! In a broken time blur of words I try to communicate to Sky. I'm nervously eyeballing the Flyen's back door that is right next to the bathroom. She'll never know, sitting here she looks so innocently and beautiful. She is a total distraction, I'm on a mission and the longer she's with me the greater chance she has of getting hurt or losing her mind. Not till after I eat my burrito, then I'll run for it! I convince myself this is for the best and I have no way around it.

"UMMm, ah yes, the chicken, guacamole, jalapeño, sour cream, red beans and rice burrito please." I order with my mouth watering. Sky asking me what she should order, only confirming my beliefs that this is way to heavy of an operation to be drugging this unsuspecting girl around. How much have I told her in my confessions? I never showed her where I'll be staying, but I did mention it was Third Street off St. Charles? She'll rip my lungs out if she finds me after I abandon her. Now more than ever I'm obsessing over the thought of the alligator hat. It'll be my cover, guarding me from bad mojo. The gator will handle my other worldly battles and free my focus to the "Here and Now!" I say out loud.

"What was that?" Sky asks.

My eyes darting from Sky's to avoid contact. I say, "Here and now, where's our waitress? I want our burritos here and now." That was a close one, I almost gave my flight away. The waitress part covered my darting eyes. My beer is empty and so is my stomach.

After the nourishing meal I give the waitress $30 bucks and tell Sky that I've got to use the bathroom. Opening the door the sun bursts into the smoke filled room, shooting my nerves to a 100' tall but Sky doesn't even notice as her attention is absorbing the artwork on the walls that is shifting on the walls before her hallucinating eyes. I turn away from her and step out. I am immediately engulfed in light and I feel the chains fall from me as angels lift my spirits.

Escaping feels so great that I burst into a run while letting off sounds uncharacteristic of a human being. In the restaurant I am sure that the confused waitress tells Sky she saw me scurrying down the street… Yelling I am free!

A clean get away. I really loved that girl, I know terrible to abandon her but I know that leaving her was for the best. Sky was far too innocent and more than a glimpse of my insanity would have ruined her for life. She still has a chance that a seed will grow in her mind of wanderlust and searching out the mysteries of life but what is, is! I is needing a gator hat to devour all my bad Mojo so I head for the bayou.

Where are you, you freak of a human being? Living out in the swamps amongst the gators and other reptiles. I have knocked off the drive in a trance like state and now the roads are no longer paved. I've been driving for only god knows how long, am I lost? I could become someone's stew, a witch doctors keychain, a shrunken head charm! Fuck, I should have never left the city of New Orleans. My skin is starting to crawl and the flock of insects are actually flyen faster than me! Every swamp noise is pulsing in a rhythmic harmony with my madness as my rubber mind bends and twists.

Low and behold a wooden sign hanging from below a mailbox. Brakes and then reverse! A cloud of dust overtakes me and I got to give this goddamn dust a minute to clear. Holy fuck, I cannot read nothing from my scratchy eyes. I hop out and take the sign in my hands. I blow the dust off it and read: Emmett True's. Sweet Jesus, I've found it!

Emmett True's at last and its getting near sunset. Remembering the pitch of the get here early from the leather mask store clerk, I say thank god I'm here now. On and on the driveway goes till I reach a clearing with huge oak trees. I think to myself, this is old family land. Smokes rising from behind an old bat and board house that sits 4' off the ground on old telephone poles. It has a rusting metal roof with a porch that runs all 360 degrees around the house. A barking hound dog is clearing the dust out of its lungs at me. Emmett's living good out here away from the world, yet so close to New Orleans.

The dog has announced my arrival. I can smell the distinct aroma of southern cooking. The burrito is long processed through my furnace and it sure smells good! The front door opens and a heavily seeped southern accent yells "wily to stop barking!" Emmett looks about 50 with a strange mix of characteristics about him on his stone face.

"Well get on out and tell me what you want." Emmett says.

"Howdy fella, I was sent here by some friends. I was told you'd have some gator skins, or be the most likely to."

"Wha'd ya come fer, all the way out here fer? There's everything at all-em souvenir stops along the road."

"Well you don't understand, I'm looking to get me an alligator hat, you see." I say

"Oh now that's something special."

"Sure smells good. What are you cooking?"

"Got me on a fresh pot of gator gumbo it's fresh and ready to eat. I'm just fixing to eat, you hungry?"

"Sure, I would love to join you." Making my way up past the hound dog I open the screen door to find a lifetime worth of oddities that take up every square inch of the walls, and the ceiling like a true Americana treasure.

"Your house is something else. You're a man after my own heart."

"A mojo man? What you know about being a mojo man?" His left eye looks at me and makes my heart jump like someone just shined a maglight at me from nowhere in the pitch darkness.

"I definitely have a mojo hand, but nothing like yours."

"Those gator hats are powerful things. I'd better get to know you first before we commit to one of them. Here, have this bowl of gumbo."

"Man, is this incredible!" I say after taking a bite.

"It has fresh okra, gator meat, shrimp, pepper and other seasonings mixed in. Its an old family recipe."

We eat dinner and I talk openly about myself. Why be shy? There is an old saying that goes… 'You know a friend better the first minute you meet them than you know an acquaintance your whole life. I can already tell this old boy is a friend.

"I'm an old Creole. Creole is a mix of Black with the Native American, and French people. Creole is America's creation and is America's borne race."

"I really don't like where my blood is all from so I don't settle down for very long. I never stop moving."

"Well if you want this gator hat its got to be earned. What I know of ya I like and I'm willing to take you through the rite of passage but you got to be willing to do the hunting and killing of your own gator." Emmett says immediately shifting his gaze to his left eye, again I jump inside from his stare.

"I'm willing to go all the way. I hope killing this creature doesn't include wrestling it with a bowie knife and killing it before it kills me. Does it?"

"Hell no. We will take my boat, harpoon it and drag it on shore so we can kill it with-out messing up its back plate. This is going to be something to see, yes indeed."

"I was looken forward to a fight. Me against the gator! But you're the professional and I do want to live to fight another day, so I have no reason to argue."

It's getting dusk and Emmett has led us out to the boat. There's more stuff flying in the air than there is air. We push the boat down into the water and plow through the insects. I'm looking around and this seems easy enough because these waters are full of floating gators. Every adrenaline gland is pumping adrenaline into my blood stream. "I'd like to buy bottled adrenaline. I wonder if it is possible?" I mumble.

The old man and me are savage hunters on a prehistoric safari. The grass is moving and eyes drop below the water as we near.

"Over there Jasper!" Emmett points.

"Yikes! That suckers almost 20' long!"

"Might be a bit to much, but my freezer would be filled for months!"

"Here, a 12 footer Emmett. I'm feeling something about this one." I tell him hysterically as I point to the chosen one.

"Fear your feeling fear!" Emmett says. Then he gives me a briefing on how to use the harpoon gun. Its about the size of a bazooka. Closer, easy, easy, FOOSH! and THUMP! A direct hit by the back leg!

Immediately the gator starts rolling, wrapping the rope around its body and legs until it becomes immobile. Emmett tells me that the way it rolled we may get lucky because it might be unable to surface to get air and will drown and die. This will eliminate knife wounds from trying to kill the prehistoric beast on shore and not to mention, save me from getting ate alive!

We sit and watch the sky change from orange fire to twilight and make our way back to the dock. "Sure enough, this gator has drowned itself!" Emmitt says.

We drag my gator up about 12' out of the water. It shows no life but this could get sloppy. I'm worried about this creature coming back to life and taking off one of my arms for its last supper! Knarly looking beast who's sole existence is top of the food chain as a predator!

I circle the lifeless gator like a sumo wrestler. I am poking it with the end of a hoe ready to jump away at any moment! All the signs of life seem to be gone, but I'm still leery of the beast. A murky dark smell is surrounding the creature and a stream of red flows from the pink tissue rip on its leg that opened up during its struggle for life that actually took the very life it was trying to save. Alligators rule these swamps and I'm thinking, wondering, how long has this creature lived?

"Alligators life is a really peaceful undisturbed life." Emmett says as he's walking back from his house with his tools of the trade which consists of a hook knife, channel locks, a large sharp edged spoon, a jug of water and other things that are jumping around in the wheelbarrow. It sounds like a one man junkyard band of chaotic melody as the front wheel bounces over the hard Louisianan ground.

Somehow I get the feeling I'm about to be elbow deep in gator guts! Alright then, I start mentally building up myself thinking of all the rabbits, deer's, and fish I've gutted and cleaned. This is like a buffalo that is nearly twice as long as me and has the weight of a small car. I lift the tail and drop it just as fast! I am startled by some water that shot from my gator lung onto the ground along with a choking sound like I was doing CPR and bringing the beast back to life!

"You're a jumpy one. This gator killing putting you to the end of your nerves? Your making me laugh."

"I'm not going to lie, this creature has my respect and a lot of my fear with it." I say while watching him lay out his equipment on a board he set on two stumps that has become our make shift working table.

"O.K. boy." Grabbing a large bowie knife he says "This blades going to run from its asshole right up to under its neck, so that we can gut the creature and then onto the skinning. But first take this and I'll guide you along."

We wrestle the harpoon line from around the gators body. I'm a lot more comfortable now that I know the gator is positively dead. First we unclasp the line form the harpoon, then pull the poon in the direction of the hit through the leg. Once the harpoon is removed instead of rolling the critter we throw the line to one side, pull it under and do this till its easily unwrapped from around the body. It is much easier than I expected. I thought we'd be out here breaking our backs rolling this sucker from one side of the yard to the other. "Beautiful!" I say as we unwrap the last loop.

"Now its time for the not so beautiful, dirty gut cleaning part." Emmett reminds me. "These aren't nothing more than survival skills for my ancestors and is almost all forgotten now." Emmett says.

"Who'd of known I'd be out here on the bayou skinning gators with an old Mojo man." I tell Emmett.

"You ain't done it yet." He says.

I pull up my sleeves and give the skeeters more feeding ground and grab the knife.

"Come here and stretch this tarp out. Alright now this one goes here along this side. Looks about right. What we will do is gut it first then roll the gator onto this tarp and leave the guts here on this tarp. We want to be quick because its getting dark and these guts are going to draw out that big gator and every other one within a half a mile from the smell of this fresh kill." Emmett says to me.

"No problem, lets get-R-done!" I say with a sense of urgency.

I made the incision about a foot below the neck where the front arms come together. The gator skin cuts like Kevlar bulletproof armor and is real tough. The knife is sharp and I make it to the tail end in about 5 minutes with a relatively straight line. Emmett takes one side, I take the other and we spread the cut about a foot apart. I hold it open and a foul smell engulfs me! Emmett puts a 2"x4" that's just a bit longer than a foot and tells me to let go. I release the cut sides and the board holds the sliced gut apart. I take a few steps back for fresh air and notice that our audience is beginning to gather on the mirror surface of the water. As faint ripples alert me to the gators coming closer to us. In the back of my mind I'm wondering where's the big daddy?

In the past life I've done this before. Problem is I hardly remember this life, let alone a previous ones! It is genetic memory and I operate on instinct.

"Lets get a move on Jasper. Quit messing round and get over here, otherwise your going into the water instead of the guts and the deals off!" Emmett says.

"Wow there fellow, I'm ready. Tell me what to do to get this started."

"Reach on in at the middle. Use your hands and scoop around the rib cage to pull everything out. Ain't anything but soft organs in there, nothing that'll hurt you. Just grab a hold and start ripen everything out. The faster, the better."

Block the smell out. Block the feel out. Block the lazy left eye stare out and block the gators out!

Hell block the whole experience out and black out! Become an animal, a hunter, it's me or the gators and I'm not going swimming tonight!

I jam my fingers in around the rib cage and instantly things start falling out. It is still warm and by jostling the insides it feels like the heart is still beating. Must be my imagination? I've heard stories about snapping turtles hearts beating for several days after they've been dead. I could have an ancient ritual and sacrifice a still beating heart to the Gods...

There's nothing holding any of the organs in place except for the tail end of the throat and the ass. Once everything is scooped out I use the knife to cut the throat. I cut the intestine like an umbilical cord and tell Emmett I'm done.

Emmett inspects with a flash light because the stars are out and it is almost night as all the dusk light is gone. "Good job, now we've got to roll this critter over onto this tarp so we can drag it up and finish the work up in the light." Emmett says.

With the gator in place, the guts are ready to be drug to the water for an easy feast. Emmett shines the flashlight and I experience the equivalent rush of falling off a cliff. There must be 50 gators swarming around the bank, their eyes all sparkle as the flash light passes over them.

"Holy fucking feeding frenzy! Should we run now?" I ask.

"Hell no, those gators aren't coming out of the water. I've been giving them easy meals for years."

"My life is in your hands, literally Emmitt."

"You are the one who came and found me. Now shut up and grab that end and we'll set it in the water. A little further…" Once the tarp is hanging about 4 foot in the water he directs me to the back, we lift it up and roll the guts off like a kid on a water slide. We drag the tarp back and lay it over the gator.

The crackle of the tarp sounds like its echoing and amplifying across the water. Then I realize with a wave of terror that the prehistoric battle of huge reptilian killers is what I'm hearing. Emmett shines the light out and 15' away from us is an explosive war of gators pounding, tearing, ripping, clawing one another to get their meal. The sky is Auburn blood red and the battle rages on. How many of these creatures will die and be ate during this battle? More than one I would venture to say.

Cannibals, stampeding to become the next in line on the dinner table. There's way to many of them for how much food we threw them and now they've been lured into a death battle by what was just a scrap. I'm enjoying a spectacle few get to witness and deviously I take up a satisfaction flinching with gasps of air as the beasts roll one another around till the victors chew through the gator stew like gladiators in an ancient cannibal war. There is no pride other than death or victory.

Emmett is thrilled too! After all the years he's hunted these savages he is no less interested in watching their primeval battle than I am. With the night on us and the battle fading to become the feast of victors Emmett shines the light for us to go toward the fire.

"Swamp stew on the bayou." He says with a chuckle. "Let's pull this gator up by the porch so we can see and get it removed from the line of hungry gators. We want to keep this one."

After 10 minutes of grunting and tugging we get the gator wrestled to the house. Emmett goes inside and a moment later a halogen light comes on. He comes back out with two glasses and a tape measure.

"Have some swamp juice. It is made of gator blood and shine." He says with a look that goes right through me when he hands me the drink. Hiding behind myself I lift the red tinted glass and take a drink.

"You was right about the shine, but it sure don't taste like blood." I say.

"Shine and cranberry juice. You drank it anyhow. This suit will belong to you. Your one crazy son of a bitch, here's to you!" Toasting me he polishes off the whole glass.

"I'm surprised you aren't up on top of the roof after drinking all that!"

"Out here we call that mouthwash." Emmitt glows.

"I'll just call it insane."

"No, just takes the pains away. This here is going to be a long night and I need an edge to maintain."

My mind wanders off to the LSD and the voice of absurdity gains ground over rationality with lightning speed. I blurt out my proposal to trip and make it as interesting as possible to an old swamp man. I'm sure that he has knowledge of LSD and any real mojo man who catches lizards and hangs their skins from their porch is no stranger to altering their consciousness. Besides this late, what could it hurt? Knives, alligator skins and the Louisiana Bayou filled with hungry gators calls out for mystical medicine!

I'm reckless I will admit. A bit overwhelming, but I figure he's giving me a once in a life time opportunity and I could thank him by giving him a once in a lifetime opportunity as well. I throw the cards on the table and the joker lands face up. "There's nothing more to debate, your either willing to gamble or your not." I tell him.

PERMISSION TO PRINT "IN THE ART OF DRENNERY" BY BOB PIETZ

"I'm favoring the idea, but I don't want to see it coming."

"Alright then you go about the gator business and I'll pour a bit of my shine in your shine and

68

we will shine as we get on with the alligator." I grab his glass and pour a bit of my hardly touched swamp juice into his glass. Even the levels out and then I spike both of our drinks with 8 drops of liquid sunshine. I turn to Emmett, hand him the glass and he hands me a gator paw. We both polish off our shine, and I can't help but wonder, how does this shit happen to me?

"We're in for a ride Mr. Emmett True."

"I've been doing your work, enough playing. We got work to do. I want surgical precision out of you. Boy do you have any idea how to peal back a gator hide?"

"Why doubt me now? I'll do exactly as you tell me old guru of the bayou!"

Knives are glistening in the light as we begin our operation. Emmett has cut off both the rear paws, but says the front ones will be part of the headdress! Headdress, I light up with a glow as I

imagine the possibilities of how this will look.
Something tells me this will be more than a hat
and will be a full body suit. First procedure is
running the tape measure from nostril to tail tip.
13 foot and 2 inches give or take an inch from the
ridges that cover the back. "13 foot, what a
voodoo length!" I yell.

"Take the hook knife and run it straight down
the bottom of the tail. While you're doing that
I'm going to start on the front paws, they are more
involved to get them skinned."

Sounds of cutting through the coarse gator hide
and tearing flesh fill the air and mingle with the
rest of the bayou sounds. I'm halfway done and
in awe I pause to watch Emmett. He's pulling the
hide off the first paw and clips the bone at the end
of each finger. "This keeps the claw." He says.

Fascinating, he peals each finger back and
repeats as he comes to the next one. He lets me

clip the last two bones and I help him peal the hide off... It slips off like its buttered up and comes off flawlessly. The damn thing looks as it did on the live gator. The muscles are a pink and white at the tendons. I would have thought the muscles to be as black as the mud it calls home, but it's bright and vibrant. I go back to the tail and once I finish I help Emmett with the other paw. Once it's pealed back we peal the tail's skin off and I see things are starting to distort from the shine and acid.

"This is the best meat all along the inside of the legs. The tail isn't bad, but you've really got to work to get it cleaned off the bone and sinew." Emmett says.

"Some story this'll be." I tell Emmett.

"I don't do this for just anybody, so don't go given out my name-you hear?" Emmitt says.

I start to notice Emmett closing one eye and looking around more. Maybe spirits have moved in with the thick air? Maybe the shine has begun to make aura's glow around the inanimate objects. Trees blowing in the breeze become alive and chatter to one another. The language of the wind keeping company with the strange folk who believe beyond the known and in the mystic. I myself know all to well the power of mystical phenomenon. Voodoo spells, visiting entities, morphogenic fields, lunar madness, or plain strong coincidence all carry energy with them.

Just then, like a validation I notice a glowing huge orange moon as big as the earth itself low on the horizon. Louisiana mojo man skinning a gator on mystical medicine guided by the influence of a moon full of mystical voodoo. Leave the suit at home nine to fivers wouldn't understand this one. I imagine we would strike fear down the spinal chord of their beliefs and cause a traumatic breakdown of their week minds. Full moons are when creative energies are at their high tide and this is one full moon on the rise!

"Strong medicine, Jasper. I'm experiencing lights and floating shapes shifting and my heads connected to everything." Emmett says.

"We call it a full-tilt rocket ride on butterfly wings through a Persian sky where dreams live and the soul is seen. You have to have gone to know what I mean."

"Its like I'm watching myself from a distance." Emmett says.

Emmett pulls a saws-all from the wheel barrel and says… "I want you to lift the skin up, while I cut through the vertebrae, don't move it because this will make or break the headdress."

The serrated blade tears back and forth like a jack hammer spraying meat as it rips through the bone with a growl. The 12 inch demolition blade vaporizes tissue and bone into a mist and bigger pieces build up around the cut until it crackles through the last piece of tissue and breaks through the other side!

"First headdress I've initiated in about three years jasper. Your gonna look like an old Aztec medicine mojo man for sure! The skin will be ceremonially sanctified tonight and my friend will authorize this suit so you don't look like a poacher to the law. The headdress will protect you from evil, turning away evil spirits and devour ill will. Very powerful suit this will be for you and align you with the spirit world." Emmett says.

Pride swells through me as unimaginable levels of adventure races in my mind. Energy is surging from the creature to Emmett and through the core of my existence. I am charged!

"Fucking unreal! Thank you so much my friend!" I say.

"Not necessary, the spirits had a reason to bring you to me. It was in each of our paths to share one another's knowledge." His left eye lifting in a grateful salute to the vivid spiritual world we walk through.

"Now I'm truly blown away! The door has opened by an invisible hand. I needed this too!" I explain the nightmarish experiences I barely made it through and anticipate the journey with this headdress. The acid is strong and my sight is animated by the geometry and visions that are flashing in my sight.

Emmett tells me "I'm going inside to gather up some ceremonial things to properly guide this ritual. It may take me a minute to find them because it's been a while since I've used 'em. I know where they used to be, I'll be back." He walks through the screen door and his silhouette vanishes in the light.

I decide to take a break for a minute with a walk about. The moon looks like its spilling out of the clouds that extend and stretch far over head. I can see through them at the blanket of stars twinkling through the cosmos. I found where Emmett's burn pit is so I start grabbing up snake like branches for a fire. The moon shadow's are playen on my imagination and everything is shifting. As I gather wood from the thickets I can't help wondering what else is lurking in the thick marshland other than gators? Are there supernatural beings watching? The symphony of insects could be the backdrop music for a movie that I am playing the leading role in...

"AAAHGRRR!!!!!!" Emmett yells.

I jump through my skin and Emmett laughs after he nearly made me piss my pants!

"Good, we need a healthy fire. We have to burn these and raise the skin over the smoke." Emmett places the tools out and holds an eagle wing to the sky. "This is a sacred Eagle wing, when you wave it the ripple summons the spirit world and will connect the gator to you."

HMMM? Still rattled from the scare and trying to get my head back together I watch him work. There is nothing like a good scare to put the fear of all things holy into you! It's a sport we play of let's see who I can scare the skin off of today? Today it was the gator! HA!HA!

Emmett lifts the jaw open and cuts the tongue out of the gator mouth and it gives me chills all over. He grins and tells me that I'm to eat it as he cuts off the last foot of the gator's tail. "This part of the tail will be burned so it can grow back in the afterlife to mirror dimensions and protect the headdress in this world."

"For the love of god don't make me eat this!" I say fumbling the tongue around in my hands. I cannot help to look at it with a heightened sense of repulsion at the thought of eating it!

Emmett turns with his right eye beaming at me. Like a finger pushes it, his left eye zero's in on me with an intensity he says "You will eat it after its been cooked. This will give you the language of the alligator."

His gaze burns into me so I don't give my gut response… I've very little expectations of speaking to gators and to avoid pissing Emitt off I say "Well, very well then. Alligator tongue is starting to sound good, when is dinner?"

"There are things you have to understand. A path has been laid out before you that I don't understand so why should you? Its not for either of us to know but we must make preparations for the coming journey." His eyes shift away from me, letting go of their invisible grasp I feel like my feet touch the ground again. "Get this fire blazing. Our ceremony shall begin with the orange color in the moon as this crosses both day and night. Through the realms of both night and day your journey will transcend time and eclipse the infinite."

His words are in my head as I feed the fire his words feed my soul. Fire catches quickly and fireflies climb out into the night. Emmitt unfolds his deer hide to expose what it is he's using for this ritual. We drag the gator skin over and lay it along the fire side. Emmitt wraps the rope around the snout several times and then ties a rope on the tails tip.

"Take this rope and wait for me, we will pull together." I hadn't even noticed the 10 foot tall posts at each side of the fire pit. "Alright, pull!" We pull and the gator rises up like a surrealistic flying gator. "I've seen it all Emmitt... "

I'm amazed by everything at this point and once the gator is raised Emmett ties his end off and I tie my end of the rope off on a spike on the post. When we are done the gator is almost perfectly flat and 8 foot off the ground, out of reach from the swamp scavengers, I hope.

In the deer hide I notice shapes but can't make out what they are. Emmett is chanting quickly with words that I can't make out entering a trance state and getting very animated. He grabs the deer hide on each end and bounces the strange shapes into the fire. He grabs the eagle wing and starts waving it. The end of the eagle wing has a handle of 6 inch long deer antler wrapped in leather to hold the wing to it so the feathers are fluttering freely while Emmitt washes smoke over the gator. The wing is amazing and symbolizes the ancient as my shaman channels the mystical energies I become spirit more than flesh.

Waving the eagle wing he guides the smoke to the gator and chants mumbles and sentences... "Spirit ancestors bless this for protection." Back into mumbling and "Powers of the universe gather, pass through me, into me, through jasper, into the void..." mumbles "Guide through the passage of the living, passage of the dead, through the night, through the day" Again into erratic jabber "Protect this soul who wears this skin!"

He grabs me by the shoulders and moves me under the gator. I stand with my head back and arms outstretched. While he's been chanting smoke has gathered like a shroud around the gator and the sparks look like forms that take shape and move. Flickers of life as the formless take form Emmitt waves the smoke over my body. The smoke rises up around the gator while Emmitt chants, "Ancestors come now and fill us, guide us, teach us..." Back into frantic mumbles "Universe I move through, watch and guide this soul as he ascends through the mystic land, the shamans path of journey and destination...so it shall be, shall become... is!"

Emmett collapses and I feel like a rod of light. I'm compelled to absorb this energy I feel with my head back and my arms outstretched I feel something happening. Five minutes goes by and Emmett rises chanting "So it is DONE!" Then his eyes gazing through me he takes my hand and says "You have been joined with a spirit guide and will be guided when you need guidance, protected when you need protected, enlightened when you need revelations, and you will be visited by others as you cut through the alter worlds with the mark of the mojo hand." He releases my hand, drops his head, lifts his head up, raises his hands to my shoulders and says "WELCOME" Pulling me in for a hug I feel a kindred bond that is warm and genuine. "you still have to eat the tongue Jasper." He says in my ear and crushes the moment.

"Thank you. Why do you have to fuck it up with the tongue?"

Formalitics aside the night is young and we're just getting underway on our psychedelic voyage. We've got a huge fire blazing, a gator floating and looking down on us like it is dancing on the moon. The moon is on the rise, with moon shadows on everything. Removed from the city and out on the bayou all the stars are crisp and bright in the sky. I can always use a break from traffic lights and city life I think to myself how the mystics have gazed to the heavens much as I am now...

"I feel and see things that I have never experienced before Jasper and my swamp shine just became an aspirin next to the city shine you brought along." Emmett proclaims.

"One time will unlock dimensions to your mind and enable you to understand the extremes of existence as time bends around your visions."

"Lets take the boat out under the stars, down gator alley. First we have to wrap that carcass up to keep the bugs off it." Emmett says.

"Brass balls you have for going out in them predator infested waters. I will go because I now speak gator language. Shit YEAH!"

"I forgot about the tongue. Hope it didn't get burnt because they are damn near impossible to chew." Emmett laughs and points at me. He grabs the tongue and says.. "UMmmmm, looks just right. Get your mojo gator tongue and enjoy!"

"No you first." I with Emmitt.

"No sir, it's all yours. I've ate plenty and I'll eat plenty more. This one son is all for you." Emmett says.

"Damn-it! I had to open my big mouth. Do you have any A 1 sauce?"

No response from Emmitt but a stare so I take a deep breath, plug my nose, the gun fires in the back of my mind: GO! I take the serpent tongue and chomp down on it, but nothing! I about pull my teeth out as I yank the tongue from my clenched jaws. I have strong teeth with no cavities and could not tear a chunk off. This sucker is like rubber.

"One knife that's your wild card." Emmett still laughing at me gives me a knife but no plate. "Hey, that's good enough for me." I say.

The serpent tongue has ancient wisdom that I must ingest to own the suit. I cut it into one inch strips and then bite sized chunks, down the hatch. The hairs stand up on my back as my tongue meets the gator tongue. I can feel all those bumpy taste buds rubbing against mine and chew. My jaw tires quick with little luck like eating an overcooked oyster. My mind is processing what I am doing faster than my teeth are. This is like the un-chewable texture of an oyster the size of a golf ball and growing with each bite. This is an award winning combination with the smoke flavor of a bonfire. Thank God I'm hungry!

I cut the tongue into smaller pieces so I can fit the chopped pieces in my mouth to swallow them. Gulp, all the way, keep going, no, no don't come back up! Almost, AH-YES! First piece down! I could feel the sensation ride all the way deep into my belly. "What's that I hear, is that? No it can't be, maybe? Emmett is that an alligator talking?"

Just kidding to myself, and getting another laugh out of Emmett. The first one's always the ground breaker. This tongues been conquered and the rest will be a breeze, maybe?

Excruciating challenge, I'm twitching like some one's plugged 110volt in my stomach as I am locked in a battle of mind over tongue. I cut the pieces small enough to swallow without chewing and start making good progress. My face is erratically shifting as my mouth spasms under the strain of finishing the last few bites. Is this part of the deal, to be uncontrollably nauseous? Twitching with a loss of control over facial motor functions? The mysteries of the gator language shall reveal themselves. Insane just became more insane. I am a raving mad crazy lunatic looking out of my eye holes! Hmmm down to the last piece. The last bite is going to kill me. My shirt is soaked and beads of sweet are pouring out of my face horizontally. Head back and swallow! Aghrrrrr! My face must be green shades with yellow accents. How many bites? how many years have passed? Will this ever end? Where did civilization go? I feel primitive, primal, deep bone shudders creep over me or maybe is it just the acid?

Emmitt did this to me, I have tears of joy coming out of my eyes. "You bastard, I'm done! I'm done! I have ate the savages tongue."

I feel like my face is going to twitch for weeks. I need water! Swamp shine! Anything at this point. RUM, run for the RUM! Rum is always there when I need a true companion. Through the good times, bad times, great times, the fucked times, and the times I don't want to remember times! Like this time with that God forsaken ' Lengua del Diablo!'

This bottle is coming with me. Any more of that swamp shine and I'll be falling face first out of that rickety boat into the feeding frenzy of my grave that is waiting just past the thin aluminum wall of the boat that keeps us alive. I've got a fire in my belly, and the burn is rising into my neck. I become heated and take the standing fetal position as I begin to hurl violently. The gator tongue is causing me to vomit! I try to stop but every part of my stomach is projecting out!

I get past the dry heaves and find Emmett waiting at the boat. He says "We have 2 spotlights, extra gas, a dozen flairs, swamp shine, and a full moon let's go!"

"You sure know where you belong, anywhere else and you would frighten people."

"Shut up and don't fall out." He says.

I mumble under my breath, one of my favorite past times. The holy gates to the heavens are above and there is no separation between the milky way and us. Every last star is as clear on the water as it is in the sky and this boat has become our star ship! We are floating on the black water's mirror image of space. Gracefully we glide in the stars. The motor is a soothing drone like a didgeridoo inspiring meditation soothing my twitching face! The chopping waves sound like clapping hands echoing over a mountain canyon. I turn on my spotlight and drop it! I just burned a hole through the back of my brain, it was facing the wrong way and I burned my eyes right out of my head! Emmett did a sharp right as he took a direct hit from the spotlight.

"You fool, you'll kill us both! We almost rolled, they'd have to put alligator shit they scrape off the bottom of the water in a bag and put that in our casket. If you want to kill yourself that is fine, but don't be messing around with my life. I ain't ready to die!"

No use in saying sorry because that'll just pinpoint where I am. Emmitt is as blind as me and once we get our sight back I'll see him coming. He'll be cooled off in a minute. That left eye of his might be more sensitive to light and that blast could have felt like a hammer blow to his head.

"I'm sorry Emmett, I was hit too. How about you handle the lights from now on."

"Next time your swimming back to the shore. No more sweet talking your way out of it! You can use the lights, but its gonna be a long swim."

I think to myself, that would be universal balance, I took out one of theirs, they would take out me! Thank God it is so incredible out here. My eyes begin to regain focus and I slip back into the joy of this profound experience.

I am as high as a Georgia pine and in the absence of conversation my mind begins to glow. Reality becomes warped and looking out across the water there they were alligators dancing gracefully like ice skaters on the water. Two of them are paw in paw standing upright with their tails dragging behind them. Somehow they see me, turn and their supernatural eyes glow! This is telling me they are onto me... Just then they shot up by their tails about 15 foot, back-diving away from one another! Ripples began shaking the boat. I jump down and put my hands on the side of the boat and peered out. Nothing... no charging bull gators... no ripples... Only the sound of Emmett saying he'll give me something to be afraid of if I don't straighten my ass up!

What gives? Where did I go wrong? Somehow I know they are going to strike. I've got that feeling that I am being watched. I can still smell the blood from skinning that creature and they are all family in this swamp. The only explanation I can think of for my paranoia is an eye for an eye and the gators are coming for their eye.

"Rum?" I ask Emmett extending the bottle to him. I read his reaction carefully in this strange state of reality I am examining everything.

"Thought you weren't going to ask!" Giving a yes his eyes widen up and he takes a big chug and passes the bottle back to me.

I take a chug and break into a rant. "Old Emmett True, he's a crazy man, liven on the bayou surrounded by gator land, all fucked up under a full mojo moon, on white man medicine that he never knew. He's born and raised under the mojo hand skinning lizards and gators on the bayou! He can cast a Voodoo spell from a thousand miles away on you!" I ramble of into blither and start laughing.

"Your crazy that is for sure!" Emmett grins.

"This trip reminds me of one a few years back. I wrote a poem about it... It goes like this, on liquid music in the trees, laughing, dancing, teleporting... On the other end, the other end of a puddle!" I sing

"What you sayen, I've been puddle?"

"Yah-ser! You sure have. Ain't it a beautiful thing?"

"Here's a beautiful thing." Emmett shoots a flare off and the whole swamp lights up. The glowing eyes of life are as close as 10 feet away from us and there must be hundreds of them. "Look at all of those gators." Emmett points out.

"These things are far from going extinct." I say.

Emmett fires the motor back up and we do a big loop. I'm fucking ready for rhinoceros to surface or the monster of the swamp to rear its ugly head as he shines the light over the swamp. The glow of the gator eyes are startling, startling because there's so many of them. Heading back to the house Emmett has been telling me about growing up out here. He tells me the stories his parents told him about the Indians that still lived the old way until the 40's. The Indians taught his dad and his dad taught Emmitt.

"The headdress will have to cure properly and won't be ready until Friday." Emmett says.

"Interesting, we've slipped into a pocket of perpetual time." I gaze at the glowing orb as my watery retinas take on a vivid hallucination I guess is vortex opening up in front of us. Scientist have searched for this and I have found it here... My vision spider-webs and as my pupils dilate the orb goes dark. "What was that?" I ask.

"It's Sunday, I'm guessing 4am." Emmitt answers oblivious to my visions.

"Good, this is my church. You know the land is my sacred temple? The canvas laid out for us by the almighty is my church. If God wanted for us to worship him in buildings then he would have made his masterpiece that way. He would have created the landscape out of bricks and cement. No, the Earth is the temple. Where we are now is the cathedral place of the holy."

"My head is spinning and my eyes are filled with colors. I'm still not sure what to make of it but I like it!" Emmett says.

"Your first ride is so overwhelming as you experience a reality so complex makes you flabbergasted you might say. Let it roll, make friends with the keeper and he'll let you through the vortex. Emancipate yourself!" I say and continue into a Bob Marley tune… "Emancipate yourself from mental slavery, none but ourselves can free our mind. Have no fear for nuclear energy, none of them can stop the times, won't you help to sing these songs of freedom, It's all I'll ever have, redemption song, these songs of freedom!" I love listening to music on a trip and

Emmett is bobbing his head to the vibe. Man-o-man is he into this shine! "Go ahead Emmett sing something for me that you know how good it feels."

"Alright, how about; I'm the big chief do what is best for my tribe, got to keep everybody satisfied! Columbian, Acapulco gold ain't got nothing on what the big chief holds! Smoke my piece pipe, smoke it right-Smoke my piece pipe smoke it right!!! Some Wild Magnolias for your head!" Emmett howls!

"Right on to the real and death to the fakers! That is some true shit! Don't hold back, tell it like it is!" I say.

"I can see where the souls fly. Like the stars in the universe we are alive and now the life force glows far beyond the realm of imagination. So free, its beautiful here. I know my ancestors are amongst us. They are spirit form walking on the

water, I feel my Indian ancestors most of all."
Emmett says.

Vapors are rising up and images move in the shadows are playing on the water and move in the corner of my eye. The time-line of existence has been broken and we float through a tribe. I hear sounds of them talking, yelling, horses hollering, and children cry. I smell dust being kicked up and looking into their world a youth runs along as if he's signaling Emmett. Maybe it's a friend?

"Life is brief, existence is not." Emmett says.

Like a lion sneaking up on its prey the shore has taken me by surprise. I go to stand and fumble because my legs have fallen asleep. We slide along the dock and each of us ties off our end of the boat, grab our gear and make our way to the dry land.

The gator skins presence is menacing and I find it to be intimidating. I approach it slowly and scary is the one word to describe it! I marvel at it as we walk past and shudder. No more tongues for me! Entering the house all the shadows run away from the light. Emmett goes for the throne and I enter into a strange world. It feels as if I'm on a roulette table and all the sounds are circling me. I start speaking in tongues and laughing with strange vocabulary that seems like Egyptian or maybe it is latin?

Get Harvard on the line, I'm a medium, channeling the great forgotten knowledge of those who built the pyramids. Not worth the trouble, I'd be admitted for mental evaluation, stripped of my soul then returned to humanity confused and mentally raped with a void big enough to drive an 18 wheeler through from what went down in their padded rooms. Instead I will lead others across the bridge to explore this destination for and think for themselves.

Wandering outside of the body the spirit can get lost. Where dreams exist is a sticky world of overlapping imaginations. You can easily be outside the sub-consciousness and that can get strange, especially if you get locked out or donnot make it back in.

My eyes are traveling over the walls of Emmett's' house and I find his place to be stranger than a dream. He's got black and white pictures of early Louisiana and its' people. An angry bores head that looks like it just punched through the wall is staring directly at me. It is ready to gut me with its tusks if it can only make it all the way through the wall! A collection of roadside souvenirs line the walls along with matchbooks, a set of angus horns, signs, license plates, and the best is a buffalo head that dwarfs my body!

"You like that? My grandfather killed that himself. It is a family piece of pride." Emmett says as he sees my eyes glued to this huge creature of the wild.

"Amazing, that this creature roamed the entire continent before the 1800's." I say.

"Being tomorrow is Sunday morning I've got family that'll be over early before church. I'm thinking about laying down and enjoying these visuals while I figure out just what is going on up here." Emmitt says.

"That's cool, I'm going to sit by the fire. Wake me up when you get up if I'm sleeping."

"Will do." Emmett says walking to his room.

All wired I go out to the fire and let out an groan as I look up at the gator. It dawns on me there is 400lbs of reptile here and I'm getting hungry! The rum is burning in my gut and I feel lopsided from the mix of acid, shine, rum and the boat ride. I still have to get back my land legs because the hamster fell out of its cage and the wheel is spinning but the hamster isn't there, the gator ate it! I'm not going to stop drinking the rum so I better roast me a gator leg. Emmett did say they have the best meat. Wielding the foot long commando knife like a dangerous mad-man I lift it high and bring it down like an axe. The knife slices meat, bone and skin all just like butter. Yum! Looks like a giant lizard leg!

I find a long straight branch and sharpen the end so I can keep my distance from the fire. What a beautiful night! Why sleep now? As if being up for 60 some hours isn't a good enough reason I explore further and rig the leg over the fire. I pull my van over to the thick cover of the trees so the morning sun doesn't heat the van up and I turn on some music.

Nothing like roasting gator leg in the middle of the night. It starts to smell good and my stomach turns as hunger grabs me. My eyes are not ready to eat but my body is in charge now. I pull it from the fire and inspect the meat... It is finished!

The gator leg could use some seasoning other than fire. The meat is chewy and full of gristle. I eat it, then fall face first into my van and float off on a Persian carpet into a realm of living breathing fractals. I am taken to a place that overwhelms my mind and I pass out.

Nothing like an all night rampage...

Shaking off dusty dreams that linger I reach up and throw open my sliding side door of the van. Half dazed by the magnitude of the last few days adventure and what happened yesterday I am in a blurred moment of reality. I've went from falling in love with a southern bell to running like a dog into the backwoods of the swamps to search for the Louisiana Mojo Man and I found him!

I've bought into the haphazard way of life of the 'free and easy wanderer.' Picking the wild flowers of the imagination and nurturing the creative seeds of thoughts that grow from them. Cultivating a view soaked of the compulsive obsessions that overtake me. I scientifically gather experience of for-bidden and evaluate the strange satisfaction it brings.

Slowly the ambient noises of the bayou blend together like a million voices that lure me out of the van. I just about fall out face first as I untwist my sleeping body. The beauty of the swamp flows like a fountain that is always flowing for those brave enough to have a taste of life's sweet reckless nectar. Once your lips have had the taste strange and beautiful, sometimes glorious, sometimes fearful, you long for its mysterious confusion of chaos.

The shadows are long now as the suns low on the horizon. I feel like I've been asleep for a week and it tastes like something has died in my mouth. I walk away from the swamp to go brush my teeth before I puke.

The gator skin is gone. Emmett has been busy this morning. I wonder what freakish fun will I have with the headdress? Just the thought makes me smile. What madness awaits in that city? Those old mysteries waiting to unravel in the streets of New Orleans. Mardi Gras makes you feel like an explorer who is pushing through the wreckage of an old pirate ship with hidden treasures everywhere just waiting to be found.

I feel the itch that only N.O. can scratch with its spine tingling brass bands, Creole soul food, beautiful women, all night bars and array of culture unlike anywhere else in the world. I wont be able to stay away much longer as I can feel the pulse calling me back to the 'Big Easy!' The mysteries that mystics ponder through decades all pass in a flash of chaos as you take in the secrets of New Orleans.

"AyamoyaBaDAayAH!" Emmett's chanting and banging on a drum with bells.

"Natives getting restless?"

"It is a day to relax the way a man can on the bayou." Emmett says in a raspy voice.

"That must explain the long sleep that I had." I say.

"No, I think burning your candle at both ends can account for you sleeping through the day. Hell, I thought you'd wake up in the middle of the week."

"What would I want to miss out on that much life for? I'll get all the sleep I need when I'm dead."

"The way your living that may not be all that far off! But I'm not the one to be doing any lecturing on that subject. You know by the way I got running water. You need to get a shower before you scare off all the gators within a mile. Get in there, clean up and then eat dinner."

"There you go reading my mind. I'm gonna go lose my outer layer of filth."

Emmett takes me inside and tells me he's gonna have dinner ready when I go out. So I'm off to the shower.

"You're a true gentleman."

"Just don't let that get around, I've got a reputation to keep up." Emmett says.

Making my way to the shower I find Emmett's bathroom comfortably laid out with an un-expected whirlpool bath tub. The waters warm and bubbling from the air jets. I can't get my clothes off fast enough. Ripping them off to slip into the bubbling water like a warm spring on a mountain and literally melt as I contemplate the meaning of life.

Transmitted by the soothing water I transmit into my subconscious and ponder age old mysteries as I fade into the mist of dreams and begin following a panther that moves silently between the waking world and the forest of sleep like night over the land I follow the panther. We climb a path leading up along a waterfall with jagged rocks that overlook a thick Rainforest with bright birds flying overhead. We climb to the top amongst crumbling ruins of some ancient civilization where mystics once studied. A guru is sitting at the base of one of the pillars who has a look to him that calm and deep. He looks like an illuminated soul with piercing eyes that have the fire of creation burning inside of them and is sitting in the lotus position. His gaze guides me and pulls me to sit near him. The panther who led me becomes a shadow and disappears and walls shift up around us. The expansive ruins become a room with intricately carved furniture like I've never seen before taking shape. The ancient ruins that were crumbled into the mountain side are now gone and I sit inside this that is alive room with the shaman.

"Come, Sit, I have awoken your spirit for this."

I sit on a carved chair and feel the pulse of the dragon as the reptile shifts through the wood work under my skin and into my spirit and feel a rush…

I ask him "You knew I would find you?"

"Yes, your travels have brought you along this path through many incarnations to me and I sensed your spirit ready so I beckoned. In your last incarnation you was consumed by passion and you did not realize my call but was consumed with mortal consciousness. Now, in this lifetime you have let go of the pre-occupation with material possessions to experience all the things of which the mystics have pursued through the millennia and you will write into a great adventure your experiences for others to awaken their spirit. You have lived many lives, but this lifetime is illuminated and your spirit has risen beyond the hold. There is a far journey ahead of you before you reach the nirvana the enlightened souls seek. You are a seeker and your path will bring you to lesser beings who try to keep you from continuing but continue you will."

I make myself comfortable and ask him what enables him to exist in this transitional place.

He takes a deep breath and speaks in a slow voice that echoes the centuries of sages in his words. He speaks to me about all matter being composed of vibrations.

"A metaphysical mamba is what I call it because of the dance philosophers play with explaining the supernatural to others." I interject.

He continues with "Our souls are vibrating energy and God is all matter, all thought is energy, the creative flows from all substance of both energies and matter."

"Our thoughts are energy?"

"Thoughts and every part of your composition in this human life form are vibrations. Thoughts vibrate like the vibration of a string instrument and we tune to others who vibrate on our frequency without knowing someone you can feel a connection because of their frequency and the bond you have with that person can ascend human into a spiritual connection. Your heart is pulsing with a field of energy that entwines with the pulse of energies around you and your soul is vibrating with the energies of all God vibrations. When you are around me our souls are pulsing because I am beyond the human form and spiritual but when you are around other living beings with a heart your hearts send out a pulse and vibe together and create a vibrating field by hanging out."

He teaches me the principles of re-incarnation and I listen as the room disappears and we are once again amongst the ruins. This time stars glow brightly in the sky and I see the glowing eyes of the panther laying on a large arch that spinals the entrance of a long crumbled building or is it the entrance to a deeper world yet? Either way I can feel his pulse as his tail curls and sways in the arches opening.

"All substance has its own vibration from the highest compounds to the simplest forms. All matter is composed of the same eternal energy pulsing at different levels of intensity depending on the composition of elements that make up its form. All these are born from the most primal materials and the combined vibrations make up the intensity at which it will vibrate, our souls are the highest frequency and a tuned in person who can silence the other vibrations of their physical being can channel this primal vibration and is awoke. They can awaken others with effort but back to the evolution of mass and more about the soul in a moment." He tells me and gazes to the stars overhead.

"All masses like those stars are all vibrating through incarnations from the simple to the finite rising and falling through evolutions of their make-up. They began at gas form and then became mineral to plant to animal to man to the silence where the frequency is eternal. Through each evolution the vibrations become more intense building up to become man where they contain soul. Souls have divine vibrations that are caught within the body and mind. The soul is composed of the primary energy of creation that can best be explained as particle form. A particle has both energy and mass and the energy is always moving the mass forward. In the Soul the energy is moving us forward to enlightenment or the silence where all clarity is achieved.

There are many distractions along the physical path. The body must evolve and re-incarnate through levels of existence slowly becoming conscious of the divine vibrations we each contain in our soul. As one passes through the cycles of life they evolve until they reach the silent center of all and tune into the vibrations of their soul. They enter into a state of cosmic awareness or consciousness that allows them to rise above time and space and the cycle of life is complete. At this state we see the truth and our vibrations emanate the frequency into other human vessels as we radiate the awakening... Awaken, Awake!" He pushes me through the archway and I feel infinite vibrations... Clarity becomes infinite and I vibe with all vibrations of the expansive infinite!

"Dinner Jasper! Wake up! Come on!" Emmett is yelling and as fast as I slipped into that strange mystical world, it has vanished even faster all except the vibrations. I feel the vibrations and slip my head under the water to rise up awoken!

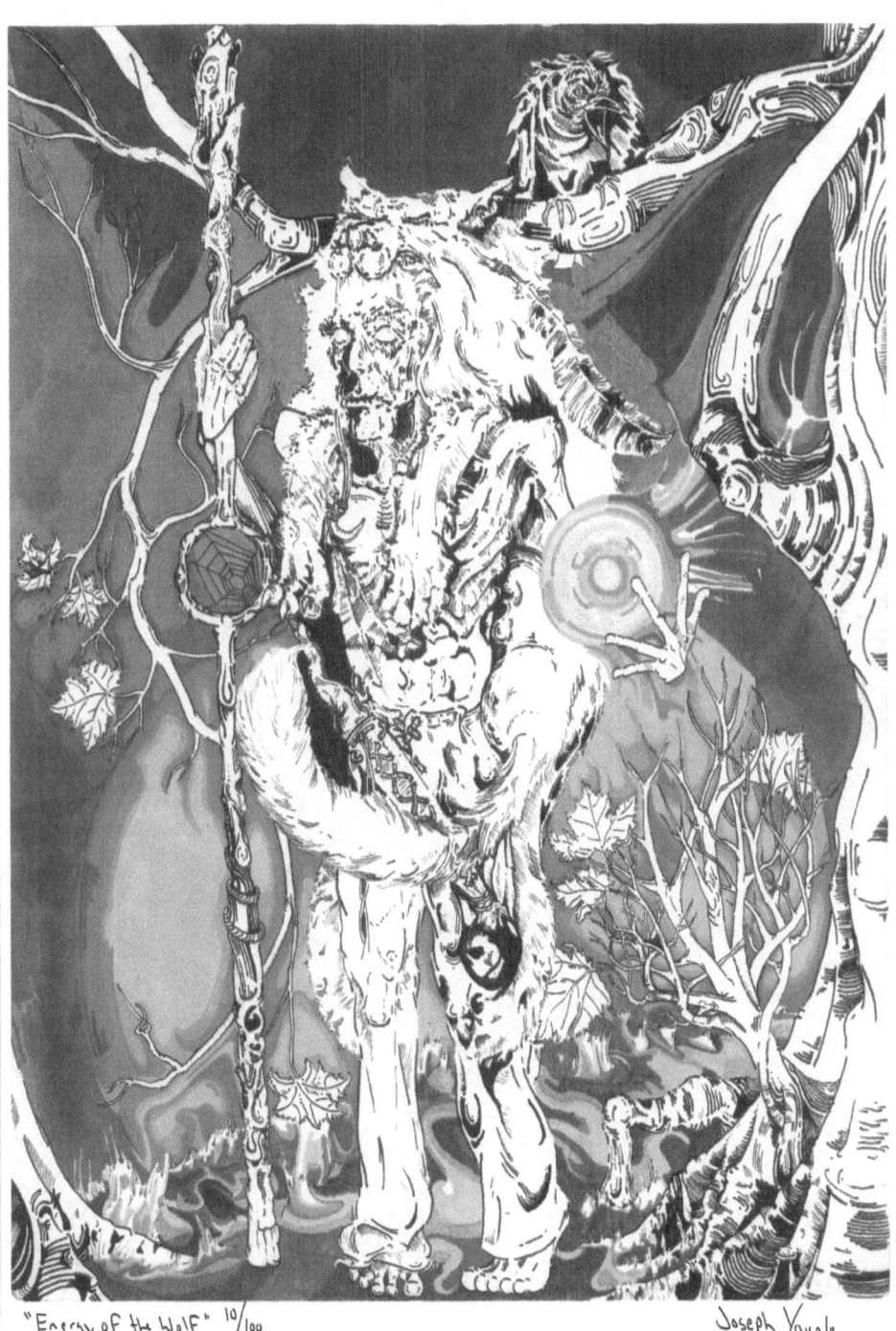

"Energy of the Wolf" 10/100   Joseph Young

119

I dry off and throw my clean clothes on. The old clothes are so dirty I ball them up and stuff them into a trash bag with their repulsive collection of swamp water and alligator guts. I shudder at the thought of yesterday. I was awoken out of the most incredible dream ever leaving one shaman for another. No guts - no nirvana! Perpetual adventure to make the awakening in this incarnation and reach the silence.

The aroma of Emmitt's dinner grabs my nose like a thief and I follow its trail to ask, "What's cooking?"

"I'll give you a hint, we dragged it out of the swamp last night."

"Gator! The fruit of the bayou!"

"You know it. I cooked it using my family recipe, just like grandpa cooked it when I was young."

The table is made up with the staples of the south like okra, lemonade, Cajun spices, and baked gator. Prehistoric meat is the main dish.

"Well don't be shy, dig in." Emmett says.

"You don't have to tell me more than once."

The gator is softer than I would have thought. It tastes gamey but I smile and enjoy it just the same.

"I still don't fully get that drug you fed me last night."

"If I have to explain it then you wouldn't understand." I say.

"Something about the experience that opened up my view to a whole new way of thinking. I'd like to go back there again."

"This is for you then. A lifetime supply." I pull out a veil of the juice and reach across the table. Emmett's eyes glisten as his dark leather fingers hold it in front of his face. Knowing the dimensional key to unlock the mind comes in such a small deceptive size is shocking.

"The gator hide is yours for this. I'll have it ready for you on Friday." Emmett says.

"Great trade! I'm more than happy."

We are both amused by our strange trade. I'm one to be in unexplainable places on a whim and Emmett's house is as strange as it can get. Once we finish our late supper we call it a night and I make my way out to my van for sleep. I start whistling on the way to scare off any critters before they scare me. The van is my vault tonight and I am the cargo. When I get to it I climb in and shut the door to keep everything out.

I slip into dreams quickly like a pirate ship out to ocean with notice to some foggy faded place behind the haze. I am running through a large marijuana crop and the calm of looking at huge plants is rudely interrupted by the horn of my van. Emmett is holding the horn and laughing hysterically at my startled awakening! "Up, Get Up! Or I'll feed you to the gators! I'll drag you out with a rope around your ankles and pull you

123

behind my boat till your picked clean!" Emmett crackling.

"Go The FUCK away for Christ's sake!" I snap back.

"Jasper its time for you to go away. I've got family coming by this morning, so you gotta go."

"Alright, alright I'm awake, I'm moving. I like you less and less this morning. Don't treat me like a bad date!"

"Good, I'll be seeing you Friday and I promise you will be glad to see me."

"I'll miss you on my way out the driveway. But don't push me." I laugh.

Once we say our farewells I pop out onto the road like the a moonshine runner. Looking for my shadow like the groundhog I about jump out of my skin when I see mine and stomp on the gas but the damn thing is following me! I get comfortable with my dancing shadow and race ahead of the cloud of dust wall that covers the road behind me.

Holding the weight of the world on his shoulders.

Wondering whether to go back to New Orleans or to go skydiving I decide to use scientific elimination of options by the flip of a quarter. Heads it's the big easy or tails its SKYDIVING! I dig a quarter from my pocket and it's a 1965 quarter. The crazy thing is I pull a 1965 quarter from a pocket full of change and feel some strange association with the year back back to the flip... I flip the quarter into the air and it makes a spinning zing sound. It jumps off my thumb and then almost defying gravity the silver orb holds at eye level for a moment then WHOMP! It plummets like a rock and bounces between the front of the seats and holds the answer to my riddle.

Swerving around a Semi I find the quarter and peak. BonZiA! Tails! SKYDIVING! The results are undeniable and I am off to the drop zone for a day of my favorite thing to do with my clothes on because the sport is a thrill of a lifetime in every jump. Skydivers are charged with a love of life and they are high on life energy from doing what they love. I feel my chest filling with adrenaline like a wild animal is clawing at me from inside to rip out by just knowing that I am about to get altitude.

In spirit with the times they are hosting a Mardi Gras Boogie all week at the Drop Zone. I've been trying to go for the last three years but each year I don't leave the real Mardi Gras until the cops sweep everyone off the streets after Phat Tuesday debauchery. I only left this year for the obscure purpose of finding myself an alligator costume on a strange mission! Seize the moment at each possible opportunity and a skydive sounds about right. I love to let my parachute air out and get some air under my feet. The view is going to be awesome over Louisiana so I throttle up to get me there!

The sky is full of tall marshmallow clouds that spiral, twist, and turn high into the atmosphere. Few things are more incredible than to climb into a million dollar twin turbine airplane, then climb to 14,00 feet in twelve minutes and jump out of that perfectly good plane. Do several flips out the door and track above the folds of a cumulous cloud to dump my chute. This will have me flying under my canopy by eleven thousand feet! And for an intense ride I grab the front risers to dive bomb through the painless valleys of folds of the cloud like a jet propelled snowboarder who can pass in and out of a mountain like a ghost walking through walls. You can feel the moisture pass right through your skin, so refreshing, so INTENSE!

I can't wait, I feel the beast clawing at my chest! Adrenaline junky's feast on one thing, raw deadly rushes not known to ordinary people. We sink our teeth into the adrenaline rush like a lion tears into a fresh meat displaying no mercy in an all primal embrace of life!

When I skydive I leave the world behind and in each second I experience a million lifetimes. The smell of Jet Λ Turbine fuel is to a skydiver like the cocaine is to a coke head! The twisting air mixed with heat and a hair raising whine of the props.

After you carve the cloud and fall through the thin blue like a hawk at 200mph you can easily lose track of your altitude. On the threshold of life and death when you hit 1,800 feet YOU better pull! four seconds- 1,300' and the Earth is getting big! 1,000'- about six seconds to impact! If your not flying your chute by 700' rarely live through it.

Sick Howard from my home drop zone and I share a joke before we jump… "Remember, if you get hurt, they give you NARCOTICS! And a helicopter ride!"

I've pulled my parachute at 1,000' more times than I'd like to remember. You look down and the trees are big! When you can tell what people are wearing you know your in trouble! Every now and then the jump is going so good a skydiver will forget all about the ground and burn in. Die doing what you love, but die just the same. 'Die a horrible death in front of cheering spectators, SKYDIVE!' The sticker goes.

On the radio the Marshal Tucker Band comes on singing "Gonna buy a ticket now, ain't never coming back. Can't you see what that woman's doing to me? Oh she's such a crazy lady!" I'm howling and driven!

My element, this, here, now is what liven is all about. A man, a van, a mission! Always chasen butterfly dreams on a mission! Following the black highway zig-zagging through America's backyard. Traveling is sacred to me and I love the freedom of experiencing the lost highways of America.

Marshal Tucker slips into the Alman Brothers ; "They call me the breeze!" The mood is right and the atmosphere is nuclear. WoW! A COP! Sitting behind a bridge shooting his radar. The tax man collecting his revenue for the man! I was just about to burn one, but the roller killed that idea.

The gas gauge is looking hit and I am about to run on vapors. My silver and blue Safari is a carnivore and the road becomes the meat, but it needs gas to wash the highway into the rearview mirror. One of the first weekends I had this van I was at Tipitina's. I drank myself into a black out stupor and somehow crawled back to the belly of my van. I entered a spinning vortex and found myself in a golden shower the next morning, so I immediately ripped the carpet out of the van and it was officially christened! I know its sick, but this life of excess isn't always pretty.

GAS-this exit. Pulling down the ramp I'm greeted with signs advertising bait, cigarettes, beer and more beer... There won't be any skydiving with beer on my breath, but breakfast sounds good. I'm going to get gas, use the phone, shake hands with the general and get back on the road... 'The Rajun Cajun Diner.' Now that sounds appealing and my stomach says breakfast first. A locally half packed parking lot tells me something worth eating waits inside. Entering the diner, sweet aromas of grease mixed with cigarettes and coffee win me over.

"Where'd you like to sit?"

"Anywhere."

"You by yourself?"

"Just me."

"Here you go, front and center for the show. You can sit at the bar. We just started serving breakfast, normally we only keep night hours so bear with me, I'm the only one working."

Thanking her for filling my coffee I look over her attractive body, mid-twenties with natural strawberry blonde hair and light skin. She is beautiful. I flash her a big smile as she passes her eyes over me. Looking at the menu the steak and eggs catches my eyes.

"What you having honey?"

"You know there is something they say about red-heads."

"What would that be?"

"That all red-heads have been kissed by the devil."

Her bright green Irish eyes glow as she laughs. The old timers look at me to see who's behind the voice.

"I'll have the steak and eggs, medium rare with home-fries and the rest of the afternoon with you."

"Coming right at you." She says.

I can't tell by her voice if she likes me flirting or not. Reading her name badge I see her name is Saxon. "How would you like to go skydiving Saxon?" I ask.

"That's something I've always wanted to do." She says with her face turning red and her eyes sparkle. I see a deep smile as she turns away to ring a couple out.

I go flipping through the USPA magazine searching for the Mardi Gras boogie ad. USPA Stands for United States Parachute Association and when I renewed my license I received a complimentary subscription. Saxon slaps the steak on the fryer. Immediately it is on sizzle mode smelling soOOoo GOOD!

"I'm married with two kids." Saxon says.

"Where's your ring?"

"Oh-My-God! I've lost IT!!!"

"Imagine that, I lost mine too!"

"Not-ugh you aren't married." She says.

"Neither are you." I say.

"Your right, I don't have any kids either, at least that I know about. Maybe there's one or two out there somewhere from a one night stand..?." Saxon says.

"That is a guy's answer Saxon. Good sense of humor, to have a kid you'd have to of forgot 9 months of your life."

"Here's your breakfast. Let me know if you see anything else you'd like."

"I'd like you!"

"Sounds like dessert." Saxon says.

I can feel my blood boiling as I watch Saxon's ass walk away. Long smooth legs with a fire in her belly. I'd like to harpoon this maiden with my pink mushroom. UMmmm, the steak is so tender, it melts in my mouth. The eggs are perfectly basted, a runny yolk, like yellow sunshine. Buttery delight with rye toast to soak up all the flavor.

Saxon rings the last two fellows up and I smile at them when they turn to leave. The smile is more for the thought of knowing Saxon and I will be alone than for being polite.

"One lousy dollar, they call that a tip!!?!"

"Your worth more than that to just look at."

"These hicks only look at fat ugly women."

"Hey- this steak is sure good but do you have anything more tender and pinker?"

"Not on the menu cowboy."

"When do you get off?"

"My shift is done with that lousy tip. I'm shutting this place down until tonight. Yours is on the house, enjoy the steak."

"Every bite, thanks. What do you say we spend the day together?"

"You're a cutesy and I like ramblers. You know my name, what's yours?"

"Jasper. Encantado, which means it is a pleasure."

Saxon wipes down the grill and I finish my breakfast. I lay a twenty on the counter and help Saxon clean tables after I eat. We flirt back and forth and this girl seems as horny as I feel. I can't help but wonder if I'm dreaming as I watch Saxon flip the open sign to closed and lock the door. Saxon's wearing the classic waitress outfit, a skirt with blue on the sleeves and down the buttons.

"Nice thong." I tell her after she bends over and produces the lovely view that exposes the top of a purple thong.

"You might get to see it if your lucky." Grabbing my hand she leads me into the back. Usual kitchen with hanging pots, large iron skillets, spoons, and knives all over. In the middle is a 5' cutting board made of solid maple. Saxon leans back against the island and we begin kissing uncontrollably. The kind of kissing that has plasma white fire! I bite Saxon's neck and she shudders with pleasure.

Clearly Saxon is in control. This is her environment and there is authority in her arms.

Sweet Jesus her hand sinks below my pant-line! I feel vulnerable in her grasp. I rub her thighs moving up to her glory. Through her panties I can feel the moist folds are on fire as we massage one another. Saxon is stroking me and I'm rubbing her pussy.

We're breathing heavily into each other's ears, moaning and sliding in one another's arms. Saxon un-zips my pants and slides them down over my hips. I'm caught up on her blouse and in her hair and things are getting messy! I'm riding and she's driving the caddy! I lift her purple thong off! Slowly I run my tongue along her calf up the inside of her jumpy thigh, barely touching the tip of my tongue along the inside of her leg to her vagina. She moans with pleasure! Her body warm and her vagina is wet! I run my tongue softly over her clit while my finger strokes her G spot. Her back arches, her hands wrap around the back of my head and I'm steamy and hot in between her legs.

"Oh, fuck yes! It feels so good! Jasper I want you on your back and I want on top."

We shuffle our position with her legs wrapped around I slip into her. So warm my eyes roll back with ecstasy. Lifting her I lay backwards and we are consumed by this crazy love! Then Saxon does it! While I'm on my back she spins 180 degrees around facing away from me. She grinds hard! I can feel her massaging her clit, trembling and moaning. I let my ego slip away, forgetting about myself, thinking entirely of Saxon's orgasm. I feel her warm juice gushing so wet, warmly riding up and down my cock, so beautiful!

"Jasper I'm going to come, I want you to come inside of me, with me into my wet pussy! I'm on birth control."

"I don't know about that." OUCH! She grabs hold of my balls and squeezes them. "OK, since you put it that way."

She moans to the gush of her orgasm, racing up and down my shaft, I get larger and larger.

"COME, COME, Jasper come, ugh, UgH, UGH, UGH!" Saxon's moans of ecstasy are so sensual that I ERUPT and COME! Filling her I feel the warmth erupt like fire. Pleasure runs through my body, over my body, making me light headed, strong, week, and HAPPY!

"Saxon."

"SHUSH." She whispers, spinning around I see the sweet glistening on her body and dripping through her strawberry hair. Her green eyes fluttering greenballs of fire between her eyelids. I let out a moan as I feel every fold inside her warm soft envelopment. A red hot mama with a misfits heart. She runs her hands along my neck and I run my fingers up her body along her breasts till my fingers run through her hair.

Sitting up we embrace one each others' sweet covered bodies.

"You can never believe how good you felt."

"Right back at you."

"That's nice." I say, pressing a 1" arched rainbow tattoo to the top left above her bush.

"You made it to the treasure at the end of the rainbow. I'm your pot of gold!" Saxon says.

"Your glowing like a soft summer rain." That voice in my head tells me use your heart for pumping blood not falling in love. Here I am in God knows where banging a redhead in the back of the 'Rajen Cajun Diner.' I bet somewhere circling around is that hick redneck cop who is pissed because he can't get his doughnuts and coffee while I am in the back doing something he only dreams of doing.

Thank god for these back road dirty little bottled up girls! Saxon goes to the bathroom and I look around feeling out of place. Instinct kicks in and I smash my clothes into a ball and run for the front door while Saxon is in the bathroom. Frantically I run through the diner. Naked I blast out like a bandit through the front doors with my clothes balled in my arms and I am caught like a deer in headlights at the sight of an old couple sitting in their car, looking right at me.

"Uh, sorry." Wasting no time I jump into my van and throw the clothes down. I coast the van backwards and as soon as I can clear all obstacles I slam into drive and jam the gas. I see Saxon pushing through the store as my tires screech into action and hope the Gods forgive my sinful ways!

Nervous nerves clutch me like a fist. With each mile I get between me and the diner I can feel each finger being released one by one slowly releasing the tension off me. Sweating I notice I'm speeding dangerously. Slowing down I can feel the pressure being released and I can hear again. It is like a helmet with a void has been lifted off my head and the world rushes back in.

I turn on the radio to static. Jumping through the stations I find Led Zeppelin 'Ramble on, the time has come, I've got to ramble on! DuDuDuDu My Baby- Find the Queen of all my Dreams… Ra Ra Ra Ramble on! Now the time the time is NOW!"

Equilibrium has once again balanced to my sick balance of normality. A successful departure from the diner with no snags but where the fuck am I? High noon on the Bayou with only fumes in my gas tank. I Squeal and peel into the 'Flyen J' Gas at the next stop. This time it is gas and directions with no diners! Chaos drives me and is my guide. There is no reason for my restless soul other than a strong affliction with curious wanderlust bent around the romantic idea that somewhere out there the secrets of the centuries will reveal themselves as I discover what awaits beyond the boundaries of mortality.

The boogie waits off I10 a little over an hour and I'll be there. The girl who answered the phone at the DZ sounded sweet and bubbly with a N.Y. or Boston accent.

Back to my van and it is full sail down that black river. I must feed the van raw asphalt rolling under my wheels, windows down, radio jamming and a head full of wander lust. High from the sexy Saxon incident I think about parental warnings and proudly smile at the thought that I am the one your mother warned you about. I am your father's nightmares and what your dreams are made of... All for the moment!

1:25 in the afternoon and on the last stretch. I make my last turn off the road and into the drop zone. Passing by the hangers I can see this place is popping with tents everywhere and skydivers are moving through the maze. By the looks of this place I have to ask myself, does anybody work anymore? Hell no! Enjoyment –NOT-Employment!

Twisting under the clouds to'Run through the jungle' by CCR. A group of canopies explode like fireworks on the 4th of July. My eyes widen, my back straightens, and my foot pushes on the gas. Gotta find a spot to park and watch these guys land. I snag the best parking space right at the front door in a spot reserved for the head rigger because that is exactly who I am, a "head Rigger!"

Hook turns, pond swoops, tandems are only a second away… "Freaks, get down! Come down from up there!" My yells get everybody's attention. Oh the ground at last, someone's coming in hot and fast! Just feet above the club house the crazy bastard is locked in a steep violent dive! Damn, just inches above the ground he pulls on his back risers, smoking along at a 100 mph! sick!

"Who's that?" I ask.

"That is Dangerous Dan."

"Man is he crazy!"

"Everyone here knows that. Welcome to the Mardi Gras Boogie!"

Here, in the midst of twisting turbine props and skies filled with parachutes my head gets light. I'm back in with my people. At home with the heroin addicts of the sky! Freaks of the world, adventurers, adrenaline junkies, I'M BACK!

The sky becomes loud like a bull charging the ground some crazy bastard planes out a wicked hook turn just above the swoop pond. Dipping his foot in the water he leaves a wave following him from one side to the other while beautifully carving the entire length of the water. He pulls every ounce of lift out of his chute to gracefully pop up onto the sandy shore.

The club house looks like a cannon exploded beads all over. Purple, gold, red, and every other color of the rainbow sparkles in the afternoon sun.

I walk in, throw my chute at the registration counter and I like what I see…

"Hey now! I'd like to jump." I tell the girl behind the counter.

"Ever skydive here before?" She asks.

"Nope, first time."

"That'll be a case of beer and I need to see your USPA card along with your reserve log. Where you coming in from?"

"The swamps." I say with a giggle as I hand her my USPA membership and dig out the reserve packing log. Last packed in… Oh-shit it is way out of date! Quickly I grab a pencil and pencil pack my reserve parachute bringing my reserve up to date while she's got her back to me. After she copies my information she turns to get my log.

"You sure look happy." She comments.

"High on life, the way you get when things work out in your favor. How's the boogie going?"

"Last weekend we put 800 jumpers out and the nights were a party!"

"Well I'm ready to liven up the week."

"Super, sign here and I'll be your witness. It'll be $30 for the register fee which includes keg beer at night and $18 jump tickets."

"Thanks, here's a hundred… spend it all."

"That's what I do best, well amongst other things." She says.

"I'll bet you do. Lets do a jump together. I freefly, bellyfly, fun jump, whatever you like."

"Maybe a wild bill."

"Yeah, lets do it!"

"Alright, here's your wristband. Give these tickets to the manifest when you jump."

"This isn't my first boogie, Gracias!"

"Denata."

The stereo's playing through some tin sounding horns strung up all around the compound. The noise is audible enough to know its music but that's all you can tell about it.

The DZ is a buzz with yelling, airplanes and canopies flying in on landing. There's a small chopper taken off that holds four. I know this is going to be a great day. I Love IT!

"Hey Dan, how the hell you been?"

"Do I know you?"

"Yeah, me and you was stationed in that SEAL team together. But we can't talk about that." I said with a sideways stare and a chuckle.

"Hmmm, yeah I'm doing training jumps. Tell them at manifest you want a jump with me and its on."

"Right on……"

"Cool man, later."

My heads spinning around like a child at the carnival with parachutes swooshing by, airplanes taking off and landing, voices bouncing all around I know I am home. There is an oasis of tents with companies doing demo jumps of their equipment all trying to upgrade your experience of flight.

Nothing rivals a good boogie with cheap jumps, an in-exhaustible supply of jumpers of all experience levels, and wild partying all night long then hard jumping all day! Drugs, liquor, sex, and skydiving… What a great combination!

I burn a spliff while I am getting my gear together. Once I am good and stoned I wander over to the manifest table where I am greeted by the flirtatious girl who sold me my jump tickets and got me registered.

"Jasper, you have to get some gum my friend." She says

"Can you smell the pot that bad?" I ask.

"OH-YEAH!" She says with a grin.

I just finished a safety meeting. In the dangerous world of skydiving we have code named getting stoned with the key phrase of 'Safety meeting.' It just makes good sense to getting stoned, getting safe. Now with the dank aroma of a grape Afghani I grew with love hugging my body, I am about to climb aboard the two million dollar twin turbine prop Super Otter airplane for a skydive.

"I would like to do a jump with dangerous Dan. Is he available on this one?"

"His scheduled jumper just cancelled and I have not told the next in line so I can slip you in on this load to jump with danger."

"I am going to get you extra safe for this one!" My ticket is in and I am about to do my first jump of the day. Life is good and I ask you, how many hours have you watched the clouds shifting in the sky while enjoying the high of your favorite homegrown nuggs? Wouldn't you like to touch those clouds at least once in your life? Be suspended in the blue sky between the stars and the earth? Rolling inside the soft shapes that play with your imagination?

I am a 15 minute, 13,000 foot elevator ride to the sky aboard the Supper Otter with 20 of my closest friends to enjoy the cotton candy skies for a skydive. Skydivers have a rare camaraderie found in very few circles. Skydivers make up .001% of the worlds population, so we are rarely unique by our very nature. Bonded for a love of the freedom we experience while we fly and are being seduced by the caressing air. Skydiving is pleasure charged with danger!

As I approach the otter, the heated prop blast blows my long hair all over my smiling face. The air is mixed with the unforgettable smell of Jet-A fuel. I flair my nostrils and breathe in deep the power of the Super Otter and mix the jet-a-fuel with my adrenaline.

Inside the plane we sit in two rows with our backs to the front of the plane. We each have another jumper between our legs and lean on one another. A big heavy jumper sucks but a beautiful fine shaped girl makes for an erotic ride to altitude! Skydiving is after all the best thing you can do with your clothes on!

We have a program at our Drop Zone (D.Z.) which is if you jump bare naked, your skydive is FREE! Women only of course, as is the way of the world. Guys can jump naked, but we still have to pay and it doesn't get the excitement of a beautiful girl.

The plane now loaded and we taxi to the end of the grass runway. The pilot runs the engines up and he releases the breaks when the wings feel like they are going to rip off! We begin our loud ground run and 2,000 feet later my body surges with energy as the plane leaves the ground. The tree tops are just below us as we begin our climb into the sky. I love the view of flying to altitude and watching the houses get small, the earth expand, and civilization vanish.

Soon the view is split between the earth and the horizon. I glance at the altimeter on my wrist, it reads 2,000 foot altitude. An altimeter reads the altitude based on atmospheric pressure. 2,000 feet is the altitude that I pull my rip-cord. I have 427 jumps and do you know which jump is my favorite? THE NEXT ONE!

I taste the acidic adrenaline mixed with the flavor of the grape Afghani on my tongue. The buzz is a calming euphoric high that envelopes my body like only homegrown can. I feel like yelling out to acknowledge this awesome immortal sensation! My mind and body are a fine tuned harmonious entity vibrating with all the jumpers aboard and the intense vibrations of the turbine motors. Every sense is alive, my nerves are activated in parts of my body that stay dormant until faced with death and then they know what life is! All in anticipation of crawling out the airplane door and letting go into the blue freefall of bliss! Just letting GO and being pulled by the awesome force of gravity on a 200mph free-fall back to earth!

I yell, "I LOVE YOU ALL!" These are my people. Edge workers, thrill seekers, adrenaline junkies, life loving freaks! Skydiving is more addictive that heroin but instead of a needle you crave altitude!

I'm feeding my sickness. My sickness for all the troubles on earth and I'm leaving them all behind. There is nothing like a skydive to clear your mind. My mind is hungry for the clouds that are towering outside the planes windows high into the sky. We are at the bottom of the thick marshmellow clouds that embellish the sky like a candy playground of light creamy confections made from dreams, fantasy, and illusion.

This is my souls siren song. Courting deaths seductive adrenaline rush and then trusting my life on a thin nylon fabric when I pull my chute! My eyes grow wide as we zig-zag between the spotted sky of cumulous clouds climbing to altitude. The clouds are massive multidimensional bubbling folds of optical illusions that I cannot take my eyes off of and I start thinking of how amazing it would be to snowboard down one of them.

We are now at 12,000 feet and everyone is

loud and checking each others gear. The earth below us is insignificant to us now. The landscape when I look down is a mosaic of forests, patchwork fields, silver rivers and mirrored lakes that will welcome us back at the end of our jump but now the sky is our domain.

Loud cheers are coming from the front of the plane as Brittany is flashing the pilot her tits to get us all more altitude! The more you show, the higher we go! In this sensual world of skydiving Brittany has just bought us another 2,000 feet of altitude! Now we are going to 15,000 foot instead of 13,000 feet, thank you Britt!

I am jumping with my new friend Dangerous Dan. At 14,800 foot everyone is near the door getting lined up to exit and looking at the red light to turn green.

"DOOOOR!" The pilot yells and everyone chimes in. The Plexiglas door is lifted up and cool air tears through the plane! I am overtaken by my primal instincts and ready to be nurtured by my muse, the goddess of the air.

Danger and I are the second group to exit. We watch the first team fall from the plane and become specks below us. We position ourselves at the door with our bodies outside of the plane we are stand up and hold onto the top of the door opening. The force of the air is powerful and it is impossible to hear one another over the wind. I initiate the count sequence with my body... Count 1: Body away from the plane. Count 2: Body to the plane. Count 3: Body away from the plane and RELEASE!

Danger and I are swept into the grace of the wind. Her fingers caress us into a spiritual experience unlike any other a mortal will know. The plane flies on as we free-fall through the crystal blue sky. Danger and I are doing mad flips across from one another as our bodies speed up we start to fly heads down like bullets within feet of one another!

Right below us is the top of a 10,000 foot mountain of a towering cumulonimbus. I fly within a foot in front of Dangerous Dan, I push off his chest and in a last minute change of plans I wave off to him. Instead of free-flying to 2,000 foot altitude with danger I do back flips on departure... Earth, sky, clouds, sky, earth flow to my brain in an intoxicating array of visuals! All at 240mph falling through the ether!

I put my arms at my sides and dive bomb straight for the summit of the cloud. I am going to plant my parachute flag of discovery at the top of the mountain and be the first explorer to walk on its white puffy world!

800 feet above the cloud I pull my chute! Like an exotic flower my parachute explodes into a colorful airship! Under my feet is a bubbling cumulonimbus that no other human has ever touched! The glory is all mine, trail blazing the

sky!

I pull the goggles from my face, wipe away the slobber and soak in the moment as I dangle above the cloud. I enjoy the visual of being up close to this land of childhood daydreams and look upon the horizon with stoned fascination. It is amazing to be so close to something that is so out of reach from the ground! Adrenaline mixes in my veins with the flood endorphins as I chart my path. I'm looking at the vast summit that is the celestial source of inspiration for dreamers, artists, scientists, philosophers, children, and anyone with eyesight to gaze upon the beauty of these heavenly formations. With the right powered telescope you could see me smiling from the zenith of this never-never land of clouds.

Carpe deim! I grab my front risers and initiate a savage dive for the peak. My feet sink into the very top wisps of white! I feel the air cool as the

turbulence of shifting air swallows me in! My
body absorbs the moisture of the cloud unlike
anything I have ever felt. It is not wet like drops
of water but is a moisture that I can feel penetrate
through my clothes and into my skin.

I carve through and around the folds of the
cloud like a surrealistic snowboarder who's been
air lifted to a virgin Alaskan mountain to rage
down the surrealistic slope through infinite depths
of fresh-powder snow! I yank hard right on the

riser to throw my body into the worlds largest half pipe! That pipe runs 9,000 feet along the bubbles that fold down the cloud.

My body goes sideways passing in and out of the cloud like a ghost walking through walls! I am the phantom Carver of the cloud. I charge a groove that looks like a white walled Grand Canyon. Travelling with lightning speed I take in the magnificent beauty of the cloud. Connected by an invisible gravity to the earth I'm perpetually plummeting along this majestic mountain. The nimbus appears thick and solid but I can pass through it. It blows my mind to pass into the cloud and be absorbed in total white then blast through its phantom edge back into the blue sky with wisps of cloud trailing behind me.

My parachute is screaming like a banshee as all my weight is hanging from the front risers which points the parachute forward and increases the fall rate to a full on charge! After 8,000 feet of intense cloud carving I am almost near the bottom of this mountain. For a final farewell I aim straight into the center and vanish into the heart of the cloud. I am absorbed in moisture and like a wet dream dripping with ecstasy I blow through the bottom of the ambient haze and materialize back into view of the world.

I scan the horizon for jumpers or planes. I see the last two jumpers are starting to land and the plane is on approach to the runway. I will be the last jumper to land because I pulled my chute at 11,000 feet and hung out in the clouds as the phantom cloud carver!

My ride is not over yet. I start doing 360's to burn off the remaining altitude-FAST! My body is almost above the parachute and I can feel my skin pulling off my bones from the G forces as I fall out of the sky.

At 400 feet I start to line up to buzz the club house. I go into a ferocious front riser nose dive and charge the earth. The earth is not forgiving, but is just as tempting to charge as the clouds. I am aiming for the roof of the club house and every molecule of my being is working as one. My mind is calculating my fall rate with forward trajectory to determine my forward slope and land on spot. I have to be 100% on because the landing I'm planning has ZERO tolerance for error!

At 150 feet above the ground I do my last turn to build up speed and eat up 100 foot of altitude. In several face pealing seconds I am lined up with the roof of the club house like I saw Dangerous Dan do when I arrived. By pulling on my front risers I can lose altitude but I can't get it back!

My chute is SCREAMING! I am 20 feet above the roof and falling at the same slope as its pitch! I clear the roof like breaking the speed limit of a freeway and it is just me and my parachute! I am 10 feet above the cars and about to be in the landing zone. I let go of the front risers and my down speed translates into forward speed, I AM FLYING FAST! At 5 feet above the ground I grab my rear risers gently feather every ounce of flight out of my canopy hovering across the landing area! 40mph, 30mph, at 20mph my feet touch the ground and I slide about thirty feet until I'm doing 10mph! Seizing every inch of flight out of my parachute until my feet take all of my weight and then I BREAK INTO A RUN!!!

Blood is charging through my veins like the water over Niagara Falls! I'm ready to pack my chute and go right back up to altitude. Like I said skydiving is highly addictive!

There is always time to participate in a "Safety Meeting" and enjoy some of my homegrown before I go back up. Safety Meetings are critical to the survival in the dangerous world of skydiving!

I know what you are thinking and YES you should go skydiving this summer. Find a Drop Zone and on www.dropzone.com and get some altitude with your gang or on your own, but GO! Not to turn you away but I have a bumper sticker that reads, "if at first you don't succeed then skydiving is not for you" and a more encouraging one that reads, "skydivers, good to the last drop!"

The day flew by and my savage demons are no longer held at bay. With the sunshine setting low my demons now run wild in the twilight. I reach out and grab the bull by the horns. I'm gonna ride the beast through the inferno of madness. I made lots of new friends today and tonight we play.

My van is a smugglers sanctuary and hidden inside it are the weapons of minds destruction. Tonight I pull the hope diamond of cocaine from deep within her cave. I go big with coke because it is senseless to do a fag line. A fag line is a small thin rail. I lay out a 1"wide by 3" long gagger that is big enough to plug every crevice in my frontal lobe and kill ALL pain!

Rolling up a 100 dollar bill I take a deep breath as I hover above this sadistic mountain of coke. I exhale and like a true fiend I snort 80% of the pile in my left nostril. Tears fall from my eyes and a fire burns like matches have just been stuffed behind into my brain. That's GOOD SHIT MAN! Sweet beads over my body and I finish the rest up my right nostril.

I decide to make friends into fiends and push people to my level of insanity. My enthusiasm is contagious and tonight I'm feeling extremely generous. Somewhere out there I have a friend just dying to do a rail of coke as long as the Mexican railroad.

I have the weapons of minds destruction with my sights are locked in on. I have a loud trailer in the crosshairs….

"Hey everybody, you got room for one more?"

"Sure do, come on in."

"I smell ganja!"

"You're a rocket scientist." Alexis says.

"I'm amazed I smell anything. I just did a nose clogging rail of Peruvian gold."

"Brag about it" Brook says.

"Yeah, where is ours?" Clint asks.

"I brought enough for everybody. Say your prayers now tuck your head between your legs and kiss your ass goodbye!"

"Ain't nobody leaving"

"Good, clear the table." I say and make room for myself in the center.

Coke can make people into something they are not usually and there is 6 of us stuffed around the table that are about to meet this other side. Beer bottles are quickly cleared off the table. Four girls and two guys, this is my kind of crowd. I think I'll scare these skydivers and why not? I've got a baseball sized chunk of coke in my pocket. We've all been introduced earlier today and formalities are out of the way. I jumped with cliff and did a fun jump with Brooke. The other three girls Alexis, Samantha, and Destiny were working on three way team jumps all day. Gasps, ouuus, and ahhsss echo from everyone as I pull the cocoa from my pocket. I chip a big nugget and wrap the rest up to keep it safe. I begin chopping rails like an oriental chef whacking up vegetables. The lines are laid out with lightning speed and eyes are bulging. Brook's got her head to eye level with the table. She is watching the mounds form and licking her lips at the sight.

"Samantha, first choice is yours." I say.

"Damn Jasp, there aren't any losers! Thanks."

"Lets play a game of only one sniff. Do all that you can in one pass and we leave the rest to see who takes in the most." I say to everybody as they mentally prepare and size up the lines.

"Cocaine championships!" Cliff says. We all laugh at the absurdity of this.

"I've got the disadvantage of going first. All though I've got one advantage, I love cocaine!" Samantha says.

"First contestant Samantha braces herself, the shot is fired, OH-OH! She's stomping on that rail! Almost there, last bit! DONE, VICTORIOUS! Sam your incredible! By the definition of the rules you've won because you did it all. Do you have any words?" I ask.

"I'd like to say that in order to achieve a better record I'd like another try." Sam says.

"Spoken like a try fiend!" Brooke says as she takes the bill. She is more modest and she splits the line in two. She makes one for each nostril and one after the other she snorts them down.

These are fat lines about a half inch wide by two inches long. Cliff takes his down and I am last.

"I don't like cocaine, I just like the way it smells!" I say before I stuff my face down in the pile. I am a one pass wonder. This time the pain is the reward. The first rail took the edge away and now I am feeding the fiend. My head feels lopsided after snorting that gagger up only one nostril.

"Yeah Mon! That's de lion's heart!" I say once I finish the yak.

"Jasper would you like a screwdriver?" Alexis asks.

"for sure, I'd love one!"

Everyone is criss-crossing in conversation over the table. We're rambling about today's jumps, where we come from, where we jump and share each other's passion for skydiving. I jump from one conversation to the next and love these people.

I've made fine new friends today. Our faces are animated by the grasp of speed. Alexis is so beautiful. She has angelic soft skin and wide eyes full of fire and passion.

"Who'd like to show me around?" I ask.

"I'll be your Huck Fin." Cliff says.

Samantha warmly asks me to lay out lines before I go which is something I was going to do anyways. These ones are as big as the first ones and they dwarf most. I also leave her with a chunk so they can keep up their momentum till we make it back.

"Here's to your health! Jump hard and live fast!" I say.

"Here's to good drugs and the boogie!" Alex says.

We all snort the rails then Cliff and I hop out the trailer to lively up the drop zone. We stop off at my van and fill my back pack with some roman candles and fireworks that I bought somewhere in New Mexico or Arizona. Which-ever state I bought them in they sell the big ones and I got spent big bucks because I love fireworks.

"My buddies would like to get some of that." Cliff says.

"Lead the way and we will blast them off."

There's a ¾ full moon in the sky and a dark star filled night. The bonfires is raging and bodies dance around in the orange glow of the flames. I'm high and just getting started on my journey. This is the way that I like to do coke… Freely and abundantly! The demon wind carries me through sanity to insanity and I don't care where I go as long as mounds of coke wait at every stop!

Cliff takes out a M-80. He lights it and tosses it outside of a camper, BOOOOM!

"What the fuck..?!" A voice freaks out inside.

"Yeah Scotty put that thing away and dress your..."

"Dress my what?" Scott jumps out... "I'll dress you with lumps you lunatic!" He wrestles with Cliff.

Our angry mob moves inside the trailer with a dank hysterical blur of shouting and confusion. Water bongs, thick smoke and kind buds go around but the mix is about to expand. These guys are from one of the cutting edge free-fly teams and I'm all about making an impression because in our skydiving community they are rock stars so I throw the whole chunk out.... Its like broken glass shatters everyone's thoughts and we gleam at the coke.

"Confucius says what?" I ask.

"What?"

"Exactly!"

Two others are in the trailer other than me and Cliff, so these lines are going to be MoUnTAinS! Once you get comfortable in a zone its hard to tear away from doing more cocaine. I've watched the sun set and the sun rise and the sun set all on coke one time. This could be one of those nights because the bull has no caution. No inhibitions carries me into dangerous realms beyond safe levels of consumption of coke. I'm now a full blown FIEND! All thought blurs except for the drug. Skydiving conversation becomes distant... I need more explosives. A roman candles fight will help distract me from the abyss of cutting out lines. The walls are closing in, the light is blinding, I need the outdoors...

"Roman candle war..?."

"I'm in, lets all go."

Bursting out of the trailer I run for my life into the embrace of the cool night. The heat leaves me and my nerves calm by the sound of crickets and the soft breeze. We run like wild Indians armed with roman candles we use like rocket propelled grenade launchers. I run in the direction of the fire and the open space of the landing area under the blanket of stars I start to get my mind back.

The nights darkness is interrupted by the first whompsh of the roman candle launching, THEN BOOoOM! We blast one another like outlaws, out of control outlaws. Holy Jesus, one of the roman candles blows just inches above my head and I am showered with sparks!

Retaliation! I'll get that rat fink commy! This is WAR! May I strike down the hand of my enemies with the vengeance of a drive by roman candle explosion.

Diving, ducking and rolling around like a guerilla fighter I find my peace again. A breath of fresh air fills me back up. I've seen the glowing eyes of the demon in my reflection and have escaped his control. Taking charge of my high, running away from walls, away from mounds of coke I run.

A glow off in the distance grows and grows and grows, then explodes just inches in front of me, showering me with sparks and clapping my ears with a bang! The hit kills me and I'm a dead soldier so I put another quarter in the slot and light another candle to play again.

We all have a blast then head for the bonfire. The fire is jumping on everyone's faces and keg beer is flowing. There's a video screen showing today's jump videos and the jumpers are split between the fire and the video screen.

"Hey Jasper, can we do another blast?" Clint asks me just as the coke has let go of me.

"Sure, lets go back to the girls trailer."

Hazard and chaos of cocaine never strays far from the mind. We walk in with enthusiasm to find Samantha and a new girl in the trailer.

"Boys, this is Anita." Samantha introduces us. She from south America, somewhere I can tell by her accent.

"Nice to meet you Anita."

"You're the reason I'm here. Glad to see you come back." Anita says.

At the sight of the coke Anita say's, "In Bolivia where I'm from I could buy that for $100. Bolivia's coke is uncut and pure."

"Tell me how pure you think this is." I say.

"The coke has a soft texture mixed with rainbow scales. That's a good sign because so much of the stuff here is crap. Whoa, I think this is good coke! It hasn't been stomped on much at all. I call this Bolivian marching powder!" Anita says.

"Bolivian marching powder! I'd like to go to Bolivia with you. Take $5000, buy a kilo and write a book about the adventure while we see who can blow their heart out first." I say

"I've been told that I don't have a heart." Anita says.

There's mumbles coming from the overhead sleeper. Someone is obviously not into coke and they are pissed we are keeping them up. Sam doesn't acknowledge them. The lines keep getting laid out and stories are told. Hours go by, enthusiasm is high. We are all high and we are extremely twisted from the mounds of coke we have done. I come up with the idea of eating a hit of acid. Sounds so right that I decide to drop.

Nobody else does acid with me but they're more than happy to do the coke. The acid starts to grow in the imagination of my mind. We've snorted the night away and all around the dz people are stirring and starting to wake up.

We get out of the RV to watch the sunrise. Somehow everyone is pulled from all corners of the drop zone through the thick mist to the center of the runway. The view is wide open and a great place to watch the colors paint the horizon. Couples are wrapped in blankets and their faces wear the chaos of the night and possibly the break from whatever substances they consumed hours ago. I'm a train-wreck and I am still feeding the fiend not aware of how twisted I have become.

Out of nowhere the acid hits me in a way I am not prepared for. I'm reading people's bodies and registering the worried looks on their faces as I pass from one group to the next.

"barry" 17/100   Joe Young

I pushed so many people to their limit and held

line for line with all of them all, I am wrecked!

My speech is jumbled into an incoherent blither and panic takes a piece of me. The sun has snuck up into the sky and colors spill like paint onto glass.

People are cuddled together in circles, as couples, and in awe at the dawn. Voices echo through the mist as I begin to crave insanely for another line of coke. I have to wander through these people in a twisted state. Everyone here knows each other. We are the freaks who danced with the devil around the stars and in the shadows of the moonlight we bent our minds.

Cliff finds me in my perilous state and he tells me about his friend who wants to do a few rails that is getting on the road and driving back to Chicago. I grasp onto the thought of more cocaine is the answer, another rail and I will be alright.?! We head over to their camp and at this point I have become an overnight legend. I feel strange and come up with an idea that just isn't right.

"I want to do a jump with you before you leave. We'll call it the baby-sitter skydive. I'm so fucked up that I need you to assist me to make sure I pull my chute, THE VISUAL WILL BE GREAT! Two of you will jump with me because I need one on each side to make sure I pull my chute." I say.

Two people have a girl wrapped in a blanket and I can tell they are consoling her that she will be fine. I cannot make out who she is and I wonder if I have done this to her?

Nobody says nothing at least about the jump. I'm out of my mind at this point and they are hiding how shocked they are because they want more coke. We're sitting amongst the trees in the R.V. camp and Brooke brings a 3 foot round mirror out of her camper. She sets it on the ground in the middle of us and I pull out what's left of the coke. Everyone's eyes light up because of the amount and the sheer lack of discretion I have. It is morning and people are walking around, brushing their teeth and doing normal morning shit while we have a 3 foot mirror with a mountain of coke in the middle of it. I'm feeling nauseous, twisted, sick and my thinking is out of order.

I feel like I'm on a circus ride and everyone is reflected in circus a mirror as we all stare into the mirror while I hack out the yak. My world is melting around me as I stare into this reflective disc that is the only thing that makes sense to me now. As I regain comfort by focusing on the mirror and not the oil lamp dripping world around me somebody sits down between Brooke and Clint. No, get out of my view, not now! Fuck me this is the one I met the night before in the packing tent. His eyes pierce right through me. He says nothing and squats down at the other side of the mirror.

My mind goes wild, paranoia crushes me. Where's the rest of them? It is daylight, I can't hide. I smile and offer him a rail. He's a cop from who's cover was blown to me by a girl saying that she saw him arrived to the boogie in a police uniform.

He looks into the mirror at the coke and then at me. The angle is bad. I feel a million eyes on his face communicating in some ancient bug language. My head explodes, ice penetrates my veins as beady eyes laughing tell me he will destroy me. He stands and Brooke hugs him His stare is piercing me with ice circles and he doesn't take his eyes off me until he turns from brook and exits the reflection of the mirror. I know he's off to call in the rangers, the militia, the local law.

They're going to be coming for me in full force! I'm done! I feel the mark on my head and I know I'm going to jail!

I've got three problems besides the fact that I am totally twisted on some strange cocaine acid trip. The first is serious, I still have a $2400 hundred dollar demo chute from Icarus that I dubbed the bone crushers because it is so small. The second is I still have 4 jump tickets and feel like using them, but not in this state. The third is that I am going to jail and somehow the girl is going to play into me getting a life sentence for wrecking what was once her mind. FUCK!

To everyone's disappointment I bag up the coke and leave the mirror to find Dan. Once I find him I can barely speak. He understands my dilemma and agrees to return the parachute for me so I don't have to go anywhere near the jump club. I give him the jump tickets for his help.

With the responsibility of dealing with the Boogie staff taken care of I feel a relief, but what do I do with myself? My mind is in fear for my life and it's daylight. People are coming out of the woodwork and the more that see me the worse off I will be. If I leave now a platoon of cops will be ready to grab me. The drop zone is on private property and I'm safe here? I think...

The drop zone is surrounded by thick forest. With nowhere to hide I run for shelter straight into the thicket and go deep into the woods. I would pass for full blown paranoid schizophrenic as I visualize the cops glare in that mirror. I've done it, I've reached levels of insane narcotics and I wonder if I'll ever come down. Will I ever be normal again? Was I ever?

I enter the prehistoric realm of forest and feel my nerves calm. I know that I still have to deal with mankind but for now I'm safe in the woods.

They'd have to sick the dogs on me to find me and I feel safe. Sweat covers my body and I become animal. I'll ride the worst of this Hell out in the woods. Here I can keep unseen and not draw any more attention to my condition than I already have.

Slowly I feel the alcohol leave my system. Free of one less substance but the paranoia of the acid and cokc mixture is as real as the air I breathe and is the menace that haunts me. Feverish madness has overtaken my senses. I'm fucked up and hiding in the trees. I know the militia has been called and to the teeth with riot gear they will take me down all because I was walking around in one officers playground doing drugs in his eyesight. I saw his hatred boil to the surface of his skin. My babbling about the intoxicated jump, stupid, stupid me! There is an unspoken law to skydiving that a cop leaves his badge at home but this one wears his uniform here and I've gotten myself into a jam this time, I'm fucking done and only pro-longing my arrest…

After walking through the woods for what feels like eternity I've come out to the locals camp. In the daylight this looks right out of a Mad-Max set. There are make shift huts, tents on platforms, fire-pits still smoldering and a darkness holds under the trees so I can step out of hiding. I start to recognize the layout of camps and begin to feel vulnerable in the open. Hold myself together I repeating out loud... I am trying to hone in my speech. I see Clint's camp! I'll give him the coke, no more coke for me, I'll never do coke again if you get me through this God!

Clint, Clint I call as I burst into his trailer. It is dark, empty, cool and safe. Yes, for the first time I feel safe! I lay on the couch and pull a blanket over my head and listen to the sound of my thoughts. My nerves are so frazzled that I raise my head like a snake in the striking position at the faintest sound. I want this nightmare to end and try to talk myself down. I'm totally warped and know now that taking a hit of acid after a night of cocaine is a deadly combination to my sanity. Things would be much more different if that cop didn't show up. I might have skydived and could be dead right now instead of going to jail.

My mind is racing with vivid paranoid hallucinations and I can barely get a breath into my stiff chest. Each minute feels agonizing! I've got to get off this property, but how?

"Clint, Clint is that you?" I ask.

"Yeah, Jasper is that you?"

"Part of me, I'm glad your alone."

"What's going on, are you all right?"

"Far from it, I'm in the worst bad shape."

"You don't look so good."

"I'm fucked up, I ate a hit of acid after snorting coke all night. Things turned bad when that NY cop shifted my energy into a paranoid hell. You was there."

"That cop isn't acting any different, he's jumping." Clint says.

"Right now?"

"All day, it is 3pm already."

"I wish it was tomorrow and I was in two States over. Here, I want you to have this." I hand Clint the half once of coke and shudder at the sight of it.

"I'll hold onto it for you." Clint says.

"No man, I'm not coming back. This place is bad mojo."

"What the fuck are you going to do?"

"I'm leaving, I feel like the whole state Police brigade is waiting outside those gates."

"Your head is full of acid, you need to calm down dill weed, you're paranoid and not going to jail. The girl is fine and taking it easy."

"I'll go out in a hail of bullets! I'm a professional!" I say. I think to myself, I did have something to do with the girls shattered state.

"A professional fuck-up!" Clint says.

"I'm leaving and if they don't arrest me within the first five miles I'm going to a hotel, the first one I see."

"It's your decision."

"This has to be, I am losing my mind here."

"I'll drive you to your van. You're fucked up and I love you brother. I hope everything goes ok on your drive out."

I feel like a caged animal in my skin. We pile in Clint's truck and I sink low in my seat. I don't want to see anybody who saw me last night, or worse, this morning especially that pig! We pull up to my van and I thank Clint.

"You be careful Jasper, you're gonna be fine."

"Reassuring! Listen for the gun spray and sirens."

"There isn't no state militia waiting."

"I hope your right..?."

One of the hardest things I've done is open my van door. Stale air and haunting shadows spill out and run through the day making me shudder. My mind is certain that I'm driving out the gates to my death. Face my fear. Fear is my imagination and only my imagination. Face my imagination, fuck! I slowly turn the ignition and jump at the sound of the starter. It is strange how deranged I feel as my vibrations are throbbing with paranoia. Is this what the shaman warned me about? Getting caught in mortal distractions from reaching the silence in this lifetime? Please God...

Driving out the gates goes against every rational thought I have but staying is not an option. I must leave because if I stay here I'll be arrested for sure or worse go completely insane. I feel like a fox being let loose to be hunted by hounds. Might as well leave and go into the war zone. My knuckles are white on the steering wheel and my entire body is white with fear as I shift the van into gear!

I'm expecting to see an army outside the gates. The road blocked with snipers in the trees and a squad wearing riot gear armed with assault rifles. I Break through the gate like a thunderbolt thrown by the mighty hand of Zeus and hold my breath as I drive off the drop zones property onto the road. Every bush is the cover for a guerilla sniper. I'm vulnerable and a target since I left the safety of the drop zone. I'm sure that hater cop has called in the Calvary...

Where are you? Show yourselves! I'm in panic, nothing, not a single black and white? I don't think I have breathed since I pulled out. I am on edge and wonder, how twisted am I?

Twisted with a head full of acid and in the extremely low void of a cocaine binge come down is a dangerous place to be. I left the drop zone without a showdown and need to get off the road. At 4:20 I snuck past the man! He'd choke on his doughnut if he knew who he missed. Anywhere, I'd take a cardboard box right now. Give me a roach hotel run by a non English speaking family filled with the smell of an unfamiliar foreign food. I'm sweating like a sprinkler, my clothes are soaked and I need a miracle! Each mile is eternity as my eyes scan for a hotel I slip into a trance.

A best western! Thank you God! I pull off the highway into the hotel. I walk to the registration wiping the sweat away from my face. I approach the heavy mid thirties woman with hesitation. Please let there be a vacancy, don't tell me you are full.

"Hello, I'd like a room with a whirlpool tub."

"Smoking or non-smoking and how many?"

"Smoking, just myself for one night."

Her eyes bobbing curiously between her screen and me taking note of my distorted appearance. Her eyes are penetrating my psyche with x-ray vision peering into my mind. Get out of my head! Act normal, breath I think.

"Rough day sir?" She asks and I panic.

"Sir are you feeling ok?" She politely asks again.

"Oh- yeah, I'm on my way to the Mardi Gras. I've gotten lost and here I am for a night. I'd like a room with a hot tub because I ate some food that disagreed with me and I have terrible food poisoning."

"Well I hope you feel better after your stay because I have good news. We have a whirlpool room for $98. will that be on a credit card or will you be paying with cash?"

"Visa thank you. I'll feel better after a good night's rest."

I fill out the papers and get the key to my sanctuary. My strength is gone from that performance and I'm fading fast. My nerves are shattered from the drive and every step is now almost impossible.

Room 324, the door cracks open and the automatic light scares the hell out of me. Z-Fresh sheets, a desk, fridge and a big whirlpool tub, it's a nice room. I turn the AC on cold, start to run the hot water into the tub, pull the curtains shut and fall face first onto the bed. This is the most important 100 bucks I've ever spent! The adrenaline that got me here is gone and I slip into a delirious dream state...

Two officers drag me from a jail cell and one of them says "Your court is today." They have cold hands and cold eyes with a heinous energy about them. "When you put your list of regrets down this day is going to be in your top five!" The cop on my right says.

The cop's heads turn into pigs heads with tusks coming out of their mouths. We walk to the end of a long hallway and they kick the doors open at the end. Inside is a court room filled with demons screeching and laughing! Their evil eyes penetrate me and distorted figures fill the rows. I try to make out what they are other than pure menacing evil and when I look up they go into a frenzy.

At the bench the Judge is yelling… "Madness in the courtroom! INTOLERANCE! I! I! I! WILL NOT ALLOW JUSTICE IN THIS COURTROOM!"

The prosecutor sharpens his teeth with a chainsaw at his desk. He puts the chainsaw down only to bite into the soft of my neck ripping at my spine and I become paralyzed. This bite leaves me defenseless as they unleash terrible atrocities upon me.

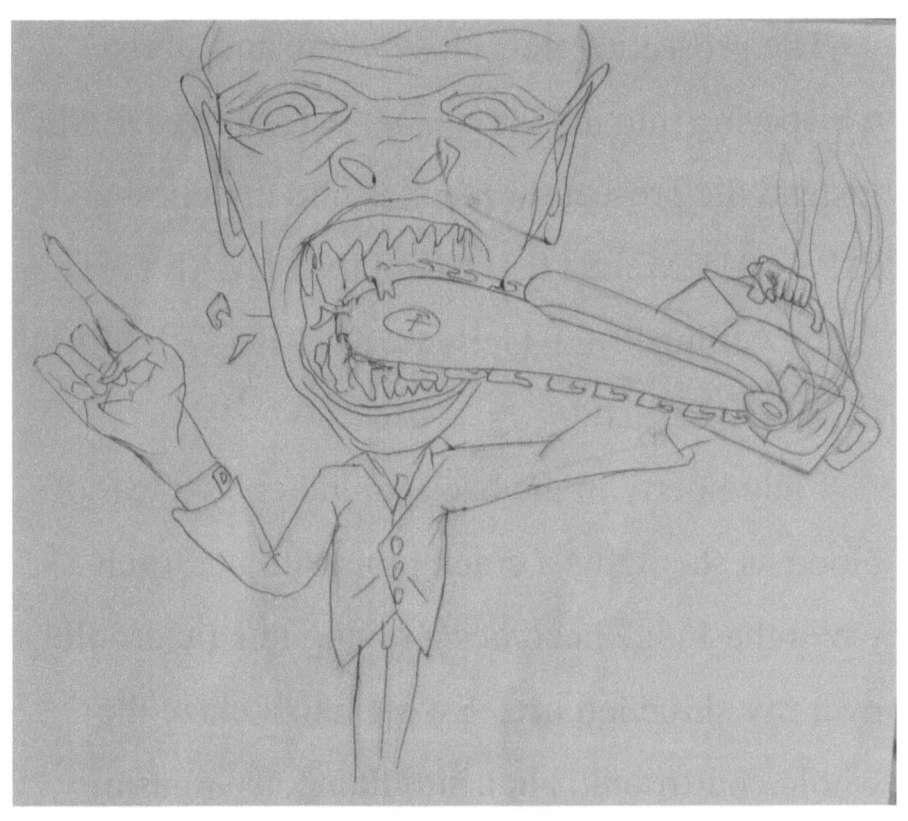

The judge is humping my leg screaming
GUILTY! GUILTY! While the prosecutor's
licking his jagged teeth my blood spills out onto
the courtroom floor from the gaping bite.

As if my blood and flesh weren't enough my
Attorney starts throwing chunks of my soul to the
prosecutor's bloody jaws. What hope do I have?

The prosecuter gets close to me and starts whispering into my ear to "MAKE ME A DEAL." Instead the prosecutor reaches into my chest and RIPS OUT MY STILL BEATING HEART! The Judge yelling "LET IT BLEED! LET IT BLEED! LET IT BLEED!"

Lady liberty in the background cry's a tear of blood as she lights a crack pipe with her torch while the Judge becomes a raving lunatic drooling over my shredded life. Swept into a craze the whole courtroom is in a simultaneous orgasm waiting to hear the verdict. The Judge yells: "GUILTY! FELONY OF THE FIRST DEGREE! GUILTY OF AGGRAVATED EXPLOITATION OF FREEDOM! YOU WILL SERVE TWO YEARS TO LIFE!"

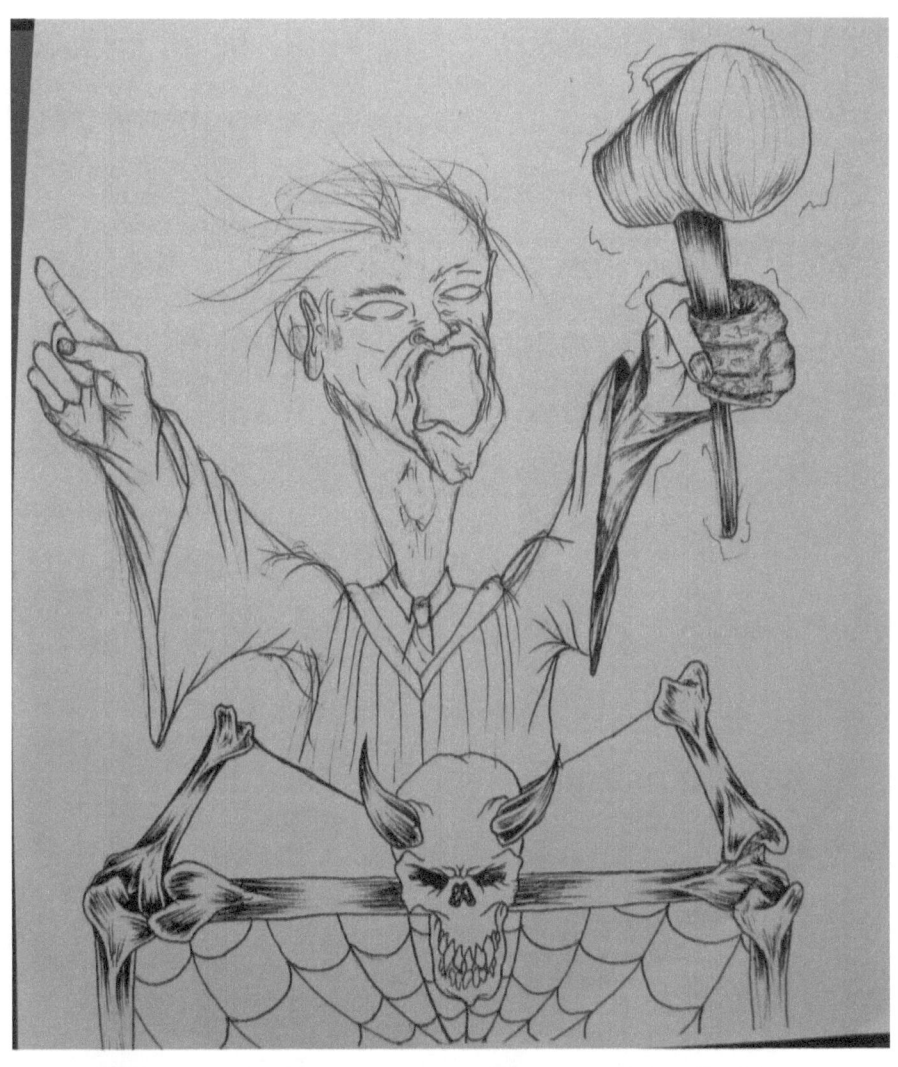

The rush is gone. The Judge and the
Prosecutor start licking the blood off the
courtroom floor getting ready for the next kill!
This is only the beginning for me on my trip into
penitentiary Hell!

"AHHHHhhhHHH!" I yell into the air so loud it wakes me up in a tight sweaty ball with the whole bed is torn apart. I get it, I get it... I look around, no-one, only me. Had I not left the drop zone that hallucination may have come true???

The air is cold now and water is spilling all over the floor of the bathroom. I grad the bed covers and soak up the water then get into the tub hit the whirlpool button and roll my eyes back. This is the best 100 bucks I've ever spent!

The next morning I wake up fine, like yesterday was all a nightmare. Thank God that none of the trauma has a grip on me today. I did have the scare of my life but now I well rested, clean and ready for Mardi Gras! Bring on the city. I am rid of the cocaine and probably better to have freaked out at the drop zone instead of in New Orleans, that would have been a tragedy!

The hotel is a ghost town. I grab a box of soap and towels off a cleaning cart sitting by the exit, load the bounty and I'm gone! Great sleep and now to New Orleans!

Onto the road with about an hour or so to go. The streets are like lazy snakes slithering through the south. I've weathered the storm and now I'm back to normal in a world that is calm and peaceful after the sinister trip I experienced yesterday, it is a beautiful feeling to be back to myself and I smile like I have never smiled before!

I'm driving a straight shot to my pad on 3rd street. No stops, no food, only the radio and the smile of perpetual debauchery. The universe can be cruel so you have got to be strong if you're going to be reckless. I'm my own personal science experiment and the lesson's can be hard learned but they are mine and for the good or bad they are engrained on my soul. Debauchery can destroy a person and this is where the art comes in. In order to have perpetual debauchery you must master the art, the art of debauchery!

Here she comes, the big easy, Hallelujah! The crescent city where angels and devils exist together and create a balance of infinite possibility. No detours, I am on a straight shot to 3rd street I remind myself. The city is alive with artists, musicians, locals, and partiers from around the world welcoming me back to celebrate Mardi Gras with them. Nothing like the garden district's warm embrace with old houses and ancient trees that line the street it is unlike anywhere else in the world. Down the center between the road a street trolley moves like a Narlin's breeze and is packed with people. I can see their animated faces and engaged minds as they hang their arms out the open windows and take in the beauty of the city.

I'm listening to New Orleans Jazz and Heritage station WWOZ playing the 'Dirty Dozen Brass Band's' version of 'My feet don't fail me now.' The sun's shining on the city as if it's telling me "Welcome back." Feels like a lifetime ago that I left the comfort of these old streets and it feels great to be back in her embrace.

The sweet smell of the magnolias fill the air. I rent what is known as a 'mother in law' in the back yard of a million dollar home. My mother in law is 3rd Street St. right off Charles in the very heart of the Garden District. They call them mother in laws because they are detached houses that a mother in law can live in without totally driving their kids crazy. Mine looks like a small ranch with an open air grill area under a covered roof. There is a small water fountain that has a cherub spitting water from its mouth into a three clam shell sculpted cement bowls on the wall next to the grill area. The ranch is covered by a Spanish style roof with brick walls and the place is incredible! It is tranquility and like a remote oasis in the middle of this high energy city. The vibe it provides me is one of complete serenity.

Turning my van onto 3rd Street the old trees branches arch from one side of the street to the other side with hanging blue Spanish moss that drops beautifully from the old branches. These old streets are lined with mansions and old money that has been handed down through the generations.

Here at last! I've made it back to serenity! My parking spot in front of the house has been left open for me. I slam the van in park, take a sweeping look, then its overboard! Exit! Exit! Exit! I picture the blue skies of a skydive and leap out with the keys and head on into my Narlin's paradise. With the crack of the Iron gate

I'm locked back in and the world is locked back out. Back in the sweet land of freaks, the vortex of creative energies. Flowers are blooming along the sidewalk. Mother Nature has lined my arrival with rose petals and sweet aromas. I shed a tear of relief when I hear the sound of water fountain pierce the silence.

I cry the tear of the phoenix and feel the warm welcome of home!

This is my sanctuary here in the city of New Orleans. The town can wear you thin during the debauchery of Mardi Gras and continuous night life adventures. When I open my gate, I enter a calm that holds the city at bay when I close the gate behind me. I live in a vortex inside of a vortex... Pretty crazy that multi-level vortexes exist in New Orleans, isn't it?

Bliss overwhelms me and grows a smile on my face, a smile that bursts into laughter. The air is warm and dry with a blue sky and a bright sun. All is good in New Orleans and I'm going to call my friends and relax.

I push the French doors open to find the place the way I left it except for a vase of rainbow colored flowers and a note on the coffee table. The note reads:

Jasper,

Welcome back darling. I figured you had a long ride so I made you a fresh pot of gumbo. Just heat-N-eat! Clean towels too and everything is ready for you. I'll be back in a day or two.

Be Good-

Chrissy!

I'm in good hands here and I haven't ate in two days. The gumbo is going on the stove pronto! MmmMm, it smells sooooo good. Chrissy is the bomb! She is a foxy blond bombshell with all the right qualities and good in the kitchen too. She's got sugar daddies in Florida, in New Orleans and one that I know of in Texas. Her career is men and she's achieved her masters' degree! I'm sure in more ways than one and I hope to find out one day. I've kissed and fooled around casually with her but nothing more than the childish clothes on play.

I turn on WWOZ and Ervin Mayfield's "Just a closer walk with thee" is playing. Speechless performance, to hear one of these Jazz masters in your living room around the world is one thing but listening to them in the town who's pulse is where the magic lives and breathes is electrifying! My phone rings so I go inside to answer it.

"Hello."

"JASPER! What's going on?"

"Moss, I'm warming up some gumbo."

"Cool, I'm bringing the beer."

"You're on schedule, see you when I see you."

"Chow." Moss hangs up.

The crazies are calling, I love it! A true spirit lifter Moss is because gumbo always goes better with beer and friends. Hot Damn! Might as well call Fritz and get this party started right.

"Fritz, the gumbo is on the cooker and Moss is bringing the beer. What are you doing?"

"Delivering pizzas, I'll stop in when I'm in your area."

"Get yourself in my area."

"Some of us have to deliver pizzas, fucker."

"I'll order one, make it your last stop."

"You calling in the order now? I work 2 more hours."

"I just did. Bring it over."

"I'll do what I can. How was the trip?"

"I brought souvenirs."

"Awesome, see you when I can. I'm at my stop I gotta dip."

"Later." We hang up.

I have a strange thought about a certain girl. Somewhere out there on the streets is a girl named Sky. I have her phone number if she gave me her real number but I decide against calling her. as beautiful of a time we had I ruined it by bailing and it would be to serious of a confrontation. I'm all about random madness at this moment and do not need a fight.

I've got to unload some of my shit out of the van. The one great thing about my van is that it drives. Other than that it is a disaster zone of chaos with musical instruments, an old tube amp, one microphone, a memory man, hand drums, speakers and the stash all woven together by my wardrobe of eccentric clothing. Strategically hidden for legal reasons is 4 ounces of hydro, 5 veils of liquid acid, 2 glass bubblers, a pill bottle full of percocets, and a few forgotten drugs that are causalities of misplaced hazard.

I grab my sandals, the stash, a handful of clothes, more of my stash and go back to my den. The van pulled through the mission and for the time being it is a sleeping soldier. Some things aren't worth the trouble but getting here was and I think of the next adventure for a moment until my mind is centered around NOW because now is harmony.

Back in my pad Winton Marsalis is blowing through the speakers and bringing my yard to life. Just as I get the first bowl packed and ready to light up Moss shows up.

"My man!"

"Jasper, New Orleans has missed you!" We give each other a hug and pat one another's backs.

"I was here. I got wrapped up with a girl then I ran from her straight the fuck out the back door of the flyen burrito."

"Crazy, why did you run from her?"

"Fuck, she was digging into my head. I need air, space, randomness. I was gripped in a moment of terror that we would be together all Mardi Gras."

"Yeah, yeah I won't lecture yah but I will give you a beer. One girl through Mardi Gras may not be a bad thing though."

We clank bottles and go inside to try the gumbo while telling war stories and catching up with each other. The gumbo is great and the pain of an empty stomach slowly leaves me. I get drunk quick off the Abita. Abita is brewed right here locally in N.O.'s backyard.

My spirits are lifted as I tell Moss about the Hell I endured when I went over the edge. I tell him about Sky, Saxon, and Emmett. Moss's been here in Narlins smoking weed, writing a book and being lazy. Enjoying the mellow life in the big easy.

"My brother from another mother, pizza delivery!"

"Fritz, great to see you!"

"It has only been two weeks."

"For you maybe but I've been beyond the brink of insanity and lost a grip. I spent time in the void where a moment is eternity!"

"This crazy fucker still isn't right." Moss says.

"Damn that pot smells good." Fritz says.

"Here's your ounce. It is a fine mix of grape afghan, skunk, and a silver pearl mixture grown in the cornfields of the great North East. There's also a couple of big bud strains in there too."

"This'll cover your pizza."

"For the next month!"

"I'm glad you guys have pot because I'm out."

"Moss, your always stoned out-of-your mind." Fritz says.

"Weed this good, I can always smoke more."

We smoke for a while and catch on helluva buzz. When we become comfortably stoned Fritz offers to drive us to Tulane Park and climb the giant oak tree or watch the barges go down the muddy Mississippi river across the horizon. Climbing the Oak Tree is ritual that I like to make a daily one if at all possible. There aren't many 800 years old trees with branches that stretch to the ground from 40 foot high that you can walk right up to the trees canopy that I know of but Tulane Park has one for sure!

Local kids go out to the navy ships and steel the thick ropes from them. The ropes are as thick as your arm. It takes balls to climb high in the tree's canopy and tie them off to create the most awesome Tarzan swings for everyone to enjoy. The tree's a spiritual place and even those who come to play can feel a strong energy about it, you understand?

Rumor is that way back it was used as a hanging tree. Humans taint Gods creations with blood in the name of Justice and the mob rule drowns out a compassion for what? Blind hypocritical authority was rampant in those times and coming back on strong today! This land was stolen from the Indians then built up by slaves. NOW ALL Americans are being EXPLOITED BY the shadow government. White, black, Indian, Chinese are all being targeted by the sweat shop low pay wage while our freedom is being taken from us and handed to corporations and pharmaceutical companies.

My friends are the revolution. In our awoke consciousness we fight by scattering across the states into pockets of resistance. As we get picked off one by one our strength and exposure grows tenfold. The revolution has begun...

The park is emerald green and full of activity. Men and women sitting on benches, college kids are playing Frisbee, kicking hacky sack, painting and all kinds of other stuff on this beautiful day. It is good for the soul to play in the sun. The artist is painting the scenery to capture the essence of life on this day on canvas for generations to see. We turn the corner and the magnificently outstretched arms of the oak tree call us to climb and smoke on its branches. Three circles of youths are sitting on the grass but no one is climbing the tree so we have the oak to ourselves.

There's two ship ropes hanging from the high branches and we full out race to the tree. Moss is the first one and he walks up one of the branches, I climb a rope and Fritz follows Moss. We all meet to the sweet smell of ganja in the canopy of the tree. Marijuana never was so tasty as it is here on this day at this moment!

Smoking dope high in the tree I feel like we are cheetahs relaxing in the branches. The Oak is right along the New Orleans Zoo and as the train goes around all the animals cry out giving you the I feeling like you are on safari. A classic laid back day of smoken weed and climbing trees. We are saving our energy for chasing girls and dancing at the bar whose musicians lures us in. Happiness, a Buddhist nirvana, a pagans church, the ancient tree is a shrine worshipped by the Druids of today, a warlocks embrace of nature. My place of Zen and time slips by like clouds in the sky.

"You know this planets moving 60,000 mph through the universe? We're always moving even while we're standing still!"

"Life, you ever think about life on another planet?"

"Always."

"I've got a theory… say this, think about the mathematical equation of heat that out star the sun creates and then take the figure of the distance.

Now take those two figures and say anywhere in the universe either of those two figures can change as long as the heat / distance ratio balance out to equal that of the Earth to Sun ratio. So say if the chunk of asteroid that orbits a star is farther than Earth is from the Sun, then the Star would have to be hotter than our Sun to equal the heat or if the distance of the chunk of cosmic matter is less than that of the Earth / Sun ratio then the heat of the star would have to be lessened to have the equal atmospheric temperature of the earth Sun equation."

"Man, that's deep. You are heavy winded today!"

"To quote Carl Sagan, "It would be an awful waste of space if we are the only life out there."

"Now that's what I'm talking about."

"Yeah somewhere out there a chunk of rock has to be the same heat/distance ratio as our Sun and Earth. There's a billion, trillion Quazy Zillion stars out there. One day the Star's will be as familiar to humans as the mapped out highways, oceans, and land that lead to our doors. We will know the galaxies passage ways and vortexes one day. Driven by Human nature to explore and discover we will uncover the mysteries of the universe."

"If we could stop killing each other!"

"True that!"

"I get a rush just thinking about space travel. Like the gold fish in the pond theory... One day someone catches a gold fish, holds it, looks at it, then throws it back into the water. Well the goldfish swims around telling the fellow goldfish about this world that exists where the water ends and the rest of the fish say 'NO WAY, this is all there is!"

"Exactly."

"Alright Einstein, why don't you write a book about these mysteries?"

"Maybe somebody is sleeping and we are nothing but the dust of existence in their dream world. None of this is even real. It is only a dream state, solipsism."

"You off your medicine?"

"I just like to think about the immensity of this colossal mystery."

"So do I."

"Well I don't"

"That's because if its not wearing a skirt, then you don't think about it."

"Fuck off."

"Speaking of skirts who's thinking about cold ones at Tipitina's?"

"Roll call…"

"I'm in!"

"Sounds good to me, too."

We all go down the rope like a fire pole. It burns my hands as I slide down the coarse fibers. Rope burn on the down slide... No pain, no gain!

The sky is starting to be laced with expanding ribbons from jet streaks high in the atmosphere…

"Moss, Fritz I've got one for you scientists. Why does a jet leave a white streak in the atmosphere?"

"Smoke?"

"Chem-trails, I've read about them online, they are the discharge of chemicals by the military and government."

"Maybe chemtrails although the jury is still out on that one. It is because the atmosphere at the altitude a jet is flying is frozen so when the jet passes through the sky it heats the moisture up and instantly after the air passes through the burners the molecules form ice crystals and that is what we're looking at."

"Ice crystals man that's cool!"

"I still think that's too much vapor to be ice crystals. I think its chem-trails being dumped on us to keep us doped up. It's all about mind control man!"

"Beep, beep, beep… news brief 'the vapor trails in the sky, are they ice crystals or are they chemical dumping? More on this later…"

"Clowns!"

We pile in the truck and bounce along New Orleans streets. I start to feel that magical pulse as we come along the front of Tipitina's. The front is roped off and there is a crowd around a makeshift bar outside the window. Colorful women stand around smiling and laughing under the spell of Tip's. My blood charges through my veins as the bull flairs its nostrils and thirsts for a seductive women. I feel a rush like I just punched a 6'7" tall meathead in the jaw and I am waiting to see what happens…

We pull Fritz's truck into the Save-A-Center's parking lot adjacent to Tipitina's. Everybody fills the parking lot and buys beer at the discount store price and pirates them into Tipitina's. The smart ones do and save big money over the bar prices. You get two night for the price of one! Double entertained intoxication!

We walk into the sparkling super market and enter the glowing isle of beer. It is a holy shrine glowing with a celestial aura surrounding it. Moss grabs Sierra Nevada, Fritz buys Fat Tire and I buy Sammy Smith's. With our liquid fuel we charge the bubbly girls that are dressed to kill. All the guys have their personal character tuned up in full force. There is an orgasmic vibe of horny free spirits swirling around each other. Girls are dripping with fantasy and pleasure in their thighs! The debauchery is thriving here amongst these freaks.

We pay the door man our 10 bucks and slide by him using our Jedi mind trick to not get searched. The power of the force is strong within us. The music that was spilling out the door onto the street is now passing over me like water in a stream over pebbles. The crowd is embracing reckless abandon and making primal connections between music and the human spirit. A spiritual harmony with the vibes of the music bring me closer to the vibrations the shaman spoke of in my dream.

When we dance to music our bodies are vibrating close to God energy. This is why creating and enjoying art and music is so important to life because we become something much bigger than ourselves when we connect in such a powerful way to creativity, or creation.

New Orleans is the other end of the dream, The waking end. There is a fine fault line between dream and existence, with all these dreamers gathered here we cross that line and become a heightened existence beyond the insignificant. Here in New Orleans the Fabled city of Atlantis is living and breathing, alive with artists, musicians, mystics, and seekers.

All along historians who don't understand intangible universal energy have been looking into the past, but fail to understand that the present holds the secrets they search for. Atlantis is an energy that grows like a wind carried from around the globe to blow into another hemisphere, time and place. The underlying magic is much like that, except it exists as a vortex of creative energy where fables live and exist in the people who come to the city and those who live and call New Orleans home as well. You see New Orleans is under sea level and is the Atlantis that exist in the magnetic bubble that shrouds the city.

A modern engineering marvel of pump stations and levees make this magical city possible. Mankind outsmarting nature to create a city below the sea. All the common sense in the world keeps the historians and archeologists blind to the realization that Atlantis is here, reborn like the

Phoenix New Orleans is the Incarnation of the ancient city.

I'm in the belly of this subterranean world and here life gravitates around the arts and blissful leisure. Charging those visiting and those who live within the bubble of its field with a clarity that is rare to experience. Like the fabled city of Brigadoon that appears every 100 years, floating over the desert for one night for those fortunate enough to witness its manifestation are forever blessed. Atlantis shines on in energy that doesn't die, a magic that you can't put your finger on to explain, but the fabled city lives in New Orleans.

I take the big easy with me where-ever I go. Now I'm back at Tipitina's, rubbing Professor Longhair's bronze head for good luck as I walk into the joint. The Professor played Tips every week to help rebuild Tipitinas into the musical Mecca it is today. Its tradition to rub the professors head for good luck, after all he got his name for being a scholar with the ladies and I need his blessing before I dance with the dragon in this lagoon.

The disco ball is sprinkling its light all over the room and the thick groove is moving everyone in a trance of funk of pounding piano and ear blistering trumpets. It's the native ancestral language bringing people together in a strange blending of culture. Strange and beautiful redefining existence.

This is the non commercial world that gives the people of N.O.'s their walk. Powerful and majestic, a rusty voiced Big Chief Bodalias slurs and spits into the microphone chants as old as the dirt streets under the pavement. Chants that spawned from the ancestors who yelled across the city to one another and tell the stories of the first Mardi Gras. He sings Iko Iko, dressed in an elaborate feathered Headdress. Bo Dalias dances around the stage with a pride of a fire dancer under the mystic trance, a shaman with an energy that purrs from him through all of us. I can visualize the great parade through his chants.

The Wild Magnolias are a New Orleans phenomena and the fathers of funk. They embody a collection of Mardi Gras chants and street consciousness of traditional songs. They dress up like native Americans in elaborate Indian suits to give thanks for helping escaped slaves to survive back in the days of slavery. This is a special concert, a gathering of New Orleans greatest musicians… Herlin Riley on drums, George Porter on bass and a whole gang of horn blowers and a guitar man who is ripping along with a smoking key player. There's also an organ player who is buttering up the whole place with his Hammond b3 and leslie speaker.

I'm in Heaven. All these travelers are taken away from their everyday life to release them-selves here, away from the race, the rat race. You know it takes a rat to win a rat race. Here you see how life could be everyday away from the rats!

FUCK THE RATS!

A beautiful blonde catches my eye, she's wearing fluid pants that look like they are covered in Rhine stones exploding into rainbows baiting my eyes I fall into a hypnotic trance. I half asleep walk over to the bar and get two shots of Yeager then I start dodging my way to the vixen. A true test of skill is maneuvering between the undulating bodies without spilling the shots. It's almost a subliminal game the dancers play, trying to seduce your drink from you. I'm a master at the art and can avoid the dancing bodies with hair trigger precision, like reading for landmines.

Finally, with only a few drops spilt I get to her and extend out the shot.

"I've taken it upon myself to get you drunk. I dig the rainbows your spinning." I say.

"Cheers to you." She glows a huge smile and toasts with me. We clank the cups together and SLAM! I get the Yeager burning twists and am set into motion. My hair is in my face as I dance like a savage with my tongue out and a huge smile as we circle one another to the seductive melody being woven from the musicians instruments, out the speakers and into the bodies of everyone inside Tips.

"What's your name?" I ask as I get close.

She grabs my hips and pulls me close "My name is Anita." She breathes warmly and runs her tongue around my ear. Chilly-o-s run over my body as Anita slips loose and dances along side of me. Eyes are all glowing and lit up on all the faces around us and her eyes become liquid, I can see the ocean waves circling around her eyes and the universe in her dark pupil.

There's a good crowd but it is thin enough to have our own space to dance and move. The sweet taste of Yeager is fading and I tell Anita I'm going to get another shot for us. She smiles and gives me a wink. Dancing like she was when I found her. I turn for the bar. Weaving my way through the warm faces and bodies I feel weightless as I float through the maze as if a hand guides me to the bar. The bar is lined with hip looking characters and a couple of frantic bartenders are trying to keep up with the demand. I decide to hunt Moss down for some Sammy Smiths instead of fighting for bar space. The hunger for a drunken buzz has taken over.

I find Moss smiling and dancing on the first floor. I grab my beers and make for higher ground. The bodies are talking a dirty conversation with one another and finding their frequency, searching for the same vibration in this place is like throwing quarters in slot machines, you throw enough quarters in the slot and eventually your going to get lucky!

The music is a thick bayou funk groove and the drummer sounds like he's balancing between 4 rhythms at once. I become a cobra weaving to his command. I see Anita shaking like a belly dancer with an audience of guys watching her move. I realize she too is infected by this bizarre atmosphere of debauchery.

"Your beautiful, eye candy!" She smiles like she didn't hear what I just said, but she knows. I hand her the Yeager and try to kiss her but she teases me with a tantalizing giggle shaking her finger in front of her smiling face and goes into a dance that makes my red blood boil.

Strange courtship as we dance and swing and groove the cat and mouse around each other like we are yo-yo's on a string. Our dance gets less resistant and we start rubbing our bodies together like two flint stones sparking fire with our collision. Her hips, her arms, her breast all crashing up against mine. I lift my thigh in between her legs and rub it hard on her pussy, her eyes get big and look deep into mine, they sparkle with a yellow blue sunburst of plasma fire. I can taste her sex, I want her sex and she slowly opens up to the music as we embark on a primal dance. She starts to command the grind of her pussy on the top of my thigh, then out of no-where a girlfriend of hers walks up behind and whispers into her ear. Anita then tells me that she will be back, damn it! Her friend is screwing up my mojo!

I can only imagine the conversation, stealing glances at them I try not to care. Her friend is definitely giving her a hard time because they are animated in conversation. Friends can be an over bearing jealous authority when one spots the other behaving bad. I can hear her now, you are too inebriated for this behavior right now... She obviously doesn't have the fluid spirit that Anita does. Anita's such a sweet young thing that I'm not going to let her friend run me off without a fight. I see that it will take some time so I walk over and tell Anita that I will meet up with her after a while.

Now I'm looking for my bro's and where to start other than the front of the stage? No where, so I pierce my way through the crowd into the mass of dancing bodies to the front, sure enough there's Moss with a smile as big as Texas! Moss is the happy lizard basking in the musical energies like the glow of a star on the soul.

"My brother! Man am I glad to see you!"

"Yeah!" Moss is jumping up and down like a Baptist at a revival.

It's hard to hear so we dance and listen to the wisdom of the Wild Magnolias singing 'Peace Pipe' "Now I'm the big chief do what best for my tribe, smoke my peace pipe smoken it right, Got to keep everybody satisfied, Smoke my peace pipe smoken it right, Columbian Acapulco Gold, Ain't got nothing on what the big chief holds, Smoke my peace pipe smoking it right. Now in my pipe is some mighty strong herb! Smoke my peace pipe smoking it right! Guaranteed to soothe your nerves!" Singing and howling the place is in a riot! We're all singing along to one of my favorite songs and I think of Emmitt chanting over the swamps, I pull his energy to me, to this place and cannot wait to see him again and get the alligator mask.

A blind man is being escorted onto the stage followed by a black women. "Ladies and Gentlemen I'd like to introduce to you very special guests here with us all tonight to help kick in the Mardi Gras Spirit, the world renowned Henry Butler on the keys! and a special, special women, the direct link to spiritual gospel, Mrs. Marva Wright! Please give them a warm welcome Tipitina's!" We all roar and cheer to their introduction.

Marva sings with a soulful voice of angels and Henry's got a big smile. Henry is moving like a cheetah and pouncing on the keys like they are his prey. Even though he is blind he moves with lightning speed. Tip's is like the belly of a volcano, heating, bubbling lava boils and explodes out! Marva's voice powerfully steers the helm of this intergalactic ship. One by one the musicians give the audience their all and the volcano erupts again! Uncontrollably flowing over and through everyone's bodies we are consumed in the fire of creation. The fire of their creativity blazing in Henry Butler's fingers, Herlin Rileys sticks, George's bass, Marva's voice culminating into the lava that spills through the speakers and onto the audience. Fire! Explosive! Unbelievable and the Magnolia's fan the fire.

I'm an energy cup being filled with the music and dancing like a trampoline is under my feet. Gospel is incredibly powerful music and by combining spirituality with electric instruments with the booze and pot and you have a dangerous mixture. Live dangerously, take chances, and see what happens! Then write down the rambles for some other soul as a stepping stone through the debauchery!

"High octane for your soul!" Moss yells.

"Tell it like it is!"

This unexpected spontaneous collaboration blows my mind! After five smoken songs Marva steps off the stage and Henry leads into an improvisational jam that shatters our dopamine glands, releasing adrenaline and endorphins through everybody's minds like the Hoover damn has been smashed and now the water is raging!

"Smash on Smasher!" I yell aloud.

Neurological overload! My neurons are lit up like the Las Vegas strip on New Years eve. Everything goes dark and it's me and the pianist, Henry Butler. His face turns to me and violently his hand strikes down on the keyboard! The sound spirals from the speaker like a tornado and hits me smack in the middle of my chest... My flesh explodes off my bones revealing my genetic DNA strand. The sound throws me backwards like I'm sliding on ice till I reach out and at the last second I grab the bar and in slow motion the cowgirl behind the bar looks at me as my molecules of my body form around my bones and she asks…

"Another Yeager freak boy?" The sound comes back as the DNA rebuilds my cardrum and I understand now what just happened… "No, make that Captain and Coke, Por Favor."

I drink down the Captain-N-Coke with the thirst of the Sahara waiting for rain. Cold and warm all at the same time. I love the burn that runs all the way down to my belly and across my chakras. "Loven Life!" I proclaim, slamming the glass down onto the bar. The bands on break and I'm so close to the doors I can feel the New Orleans night and I decide to go get a breath of fresh air. Like Mr. gung-ho I go blasting out the doors ready for action. I walk past a girl of such angelic beauty that she makes my spidey nerves tingle. How many millions of feet have walked through these doors to have their life changed? The air is moist and refreshing. Outside Tips, a thick cloud of smoke hangs above a circle of hipsters gathered in the meridian. Singing, voices, and percussion instruments all blend together into a symphony of chaos. I hear Moss's voice and See him in a circle smoking a joint with House.

"Jasper, you found us." Fritz says.

"I followed the blueberry smell."

"Good timing because the fruit is ripe and I am packing!"

I hit the fatty and watch the cherry glow bright red. The thick smoke fills my lungs with love and excruciating ecstasy overtakes me as I cough violently.

"Pass the joint." The cat next to me says. I get a look at him and he's got spirals carved into his cheek sideburns. "Yeah man." I mutter through my light headed haze.

The girls are wearing tight t-shirts and are speckled with glitter on their faces and in their hair, they've been dusted by the fairies! I hear states like Wisconsin, North Dakota, California, Colorado, Arizona echoing randomly in the conversation. Suddenly a loud screech distracts my attention from everything. My bionic ears pinpoint the blast location as it goes psoouch! Again like the sound of a fire extinguisher filling a balloon echoes from between two buildings. A Nitrous tank! I love Nitrous and there's a tank nearby! Pscouch! The tank teases out to me…

"Who's going to get a balloon?" I ask.

Walking from across the crowd she says "I do."

"My partner in crime, is your name Destiny?"

"Chloe are you going to buy us a balloon?"

"Sure I'll buy us a gang-load of balloons, come on star child." I use my sonar to hone in and guide us to the tank.

"Hippy CRACK! Get your hippy crack! Two fatties for 5 bucks! Increase your RPM's! Realities Per Minute!" The tank man advertises and entertains his captive audience, but really the scream of the nitrous tank is all he needs. The nitrous tank is the main attraction but he's giving everyone a hell of a show and is on fire. The tank is wedged between two buildings across from Tip's. We had to step over a crumpled fence in the darkness and entered into another universe, a universe of balloons where there atmosphere is nitrous.

BOOM! A balloon bursts and explodeslike a M-80! A quick way to loose your balloon is to tap it into a cigarette, and BOOM! It wakes you up from your high with the echo of the bang in your head and you immediately get back in line for more. People are spaced out in a world of another than this. They are in a world of their imaginations that as like a cartoon delusions and personal revelations and when a balloon hits a cigarette it EXPOLDES and sets off the atoms in your head like a nuclear mushroom cloud! A girl falls down and phishes in front of me, too much gas and not enough oxygen! She's in another world! She has slipped into the vortex and left her body behind while she discovers complex multi dimensional visions.

At the tank this cat has a hip sack on with bills stuffed in it and spilling out. He's wearing a big blue foam hat and says "HEY!" In a low nitrous voice I can see the nitrous mist escape from his blue lips...

"How much for a membership?" I ask.

"$5.00 – renewable when necessary."

"Here's a twenty, make them fatties."

"These are 18 inchers, not no pussy balloons. I'll get them to bursting size, increase your RPM-S! A winner every time! Step right up and be sure to sit down, nitrous isn't a stand up drug. SCOOOUCH!- Here's one. SCOOUCH! Here's two, three, four, five for a twenty!"

"Thanks man, we'll be back." Chloe and I take our balloons and Walk out from this broke down area. I have three and Chloe has two.

"Jasper I know the best place to huff out, follow me." She leads me bouncing with her balloon like a happy kid at the circus and colors spill out from the darkness and the world gets much bigger as the nitrous expands like sunshine over my mind. We go to a huge Oak tree that must be 300 or 400 years old and we lean down at its base. We huddle next to each other and start to inhale our first breath of nitrous, happy gas, hippy crack, what-ever you like to call it. It tastes like bubbly ice cream, ONLY BETTER!

"Intergalactic spAcEeeEEEeeee Traveler" Chloe says in a low husky nitrous voice. Nitrous does the opposite than helium to your voice. Instead of the high mouse voice of helium you have the low muffled voice of a cyborg on nitrous.

"Wow! Say that again, your voice sounds so sexy as it echoes inside my head."

"Our kinky machine has landed here in this strange land." Chloe says.

VVvvvvvvvvVVVvrrrRRRrrrRRRRrrrmmMMM !!! I make a space ship sound.

Our laughter is slow, distorted, stoned. There is some beautiful stuff happening. I feel groovy and I feel a connected love to everything like I am pulled from the center to every distant part of this groovy high.

Everybody doing nitrous experiences the strange phenomena of hearing a "wa wa wa" echo inside of your head and multiple dimensions on each wave of sound. The sound is as clear as a horn blowing from a train winding through a mountain canyon on a foggy night. The wa's are a fascinating echo that can only be explained like a mystical cavern of your mind cutting through the vortex of an altered reality where crystal resonance chimes through. Somebody says a sentence and you will hear the words in a complete sentence bouncing and echoing off the ridges through the mountain of your mind, echoing until the sound speeds up infinitely like water funneling into a drain, starting slow in the wide beginning, then the echo speeds up as the funnel gets tighter and tighter and tighter till its racing in a tight ball shooting back out your ear! You can practically see the words float like a butterfly into your head, then ravage your mind to flutter back out into space arousing parts of your mind that you never knew existed.

Nitrous is one intense overwhelming buzz that makes you feel so good you always want another one when the flash wears off. That is why we call it hippy crack, it has residual effects. It gets you high-FAST, then its gone-FAST, leaving you with a sense of awe.

"Butterterterterflyflyflyfly looooooooppppppinginginging ininininin youryouryourmmmmmiiiinnnnndddddDDD!" I say.

"JasperRRrrRrrRR, JasperrrRRRrrr, Vlummmmmzingzing Vumshumshshshshsh…"

Chloe rolls her tongue. I roll over and we kiss. In my high her lips feel so big and wet like two big waterbeds. They are the juiciest lips that I've ever kissed. Like a fierce storm on waves of ecstasy, clouds spiral around us as we lift up on a guiser of ecstasy!

We stop kissing, laughing and inhale more nitrous. The buzz is so deep, it lasts only an eternity as lunar landscapes take shape, the atmosphere alters. I would like to visit a planet that has an atmosphere made of nitrous oxide and rains gin!

Tranquil oceans, other worldly portals of the eyes peering into another dimension. I see a strange combination of reality mixed with psychic imagination. On nitrous you walk through a waking dream.

"Valumphous- Val – Val – Valumpshu- umphusiosious!" Chloe stretches the word.

I'm totally disconnected, watching lights swirl inside my head, then I take three huge lung filling breaths, holding each one in then exhaling until on the third one my head becomes a million fireflies and EXPLODES!

I'm a million lights and ascend into a world of light, it is amazing, I'm floating amongst billions of these particles of light and each one is a soul! There is infinite paths that particles come and go on and around the fringes many have gathered.

I have entered the place of eternal souls! Timeless, where past and future and present all exist. It is majestic, the place of all existence! All around an infinite number of glowing souls share this experience, zinging and uniting for a brief moment of connection. During this moment a million light years of existence is shared.

I meet my future and past simultaneously in a breathtaking stellar experience. I feel my fireflies gathering from all through creations realm, flowing back into my body, surging into my flesh I gasp with a breath of incredible enlightenment, glowing from the revelation! "Chloe, you gotta hear this, I have just visited the origin of all existence!"

"Holy GazooKAH! You've seen all that? I'm flabbergasted! I felt like somebody threw a dart, my head went back and hit the center of a dartboard! Bulls eye and psychedelic colors rippled out around me!"

"That's crazy, do you have a cigarette?"

"Yeah, why?"

"Light it up and I'll show you."

Once Chloe gets the smoke lit I take it and I inhale from the balloon and exhale out the cigarette. It burns like a blow torch through the cigarette, a nitrous magic trick of intense blue fire.

"Holy shit, that is the coolest thing I've seen!"

"Nasty isn't it! That's why race cars use it, it packs air in and makes the combustion twice as intense. Higher?" I flick the smoke and toast Chloe's balloon.

We inhale the last of our gas and come together on a nitrous orgy. Passionately kissing her wet lips I feel us morphing together. I nibble the outside of her waterbed lips and dart my hand into her pants. She lets out a deep moan.

"Hold on soldier." She says, grabbing my wrist. As my fingers slip out of her and to the top of her panties she says "Ahh nevermind." And pushes my hand back down.

Clouds part, birds sing, pixies fly around us, noams peak from around trees, dears lift their heads and a lion ROARS as we make love under the Oak tree.

There are morals, and then there are moments. In New Orleans the moment rules!

Chloe feels so good. Eyes wide open staring into Chloe from only an inch away. Eyes say things words haven't been invented for. Catching light, her eyes have a kaleidoscope effect to them. The seductive high of ecstasy is overloading me with physical sensations of raw pleasure as I fall into her kaleidoscope sensuality.

Electricity arcs between her body to mine, sensation peaks as I mount the Everest of passion and look out upon eternity!

Chloe gathers herself together. "You gave me a key to a door that I never knew existed." She says with a Cheshire cat smile fading into the colors.

"You'll have to lead us back because I'm lost in the world. I'm vulnerably balancing on the tip of arousal." I say.

"Jasper you are a champion."

"I am a freak ruled by chaos."

"Chaos is my favorite company!"

We get the leaves out of our hair and give the spot a sweep over, find Chloe's cell phone and enter back into the crowd we left a lifetime ago.

Chloe sails on the wind of chaos like a butterfly through the entrance into Tipitina's. Walking into the club is as if we've stepped into a box of crayons, a whirl of all the different colors. There's the reds, the yellows, the purples, and then there is chloe. Chloe is a rainbow blur of bright colors that bleed together and melt like a wet water-color dancing across a living canvas.

So much life and celebration is going down inside Tip's that the good Professor would be proud. Yes, the vibe is alive! Corporate plastic people are lost in their nine to five world. Not here, here we have a simple dream; to be free and easy, one with FUN! Here inside the vortex there's a beating pulse with a rhythmic drum jam for a heart, sewn together with infused funk and glittery jazz soaked in soul. The beat is pulsing from one conductive body to the next, filling us like sponges who are thirsty for the experience.

Everybody embrace each other, not afraid to be real. We're exposed, naked in our enthusiasm. Honesty can be shocking when innocence sheds its cloak for deviance. Chloe takes my hand, pulling me as we bounce through the sea of bodies. She's pulling me like a water skier splashing through sonic waves straight to the stage. I can see the desire rippling in everyone's eyes in our wake. The way Chloe moves fills me with such a dreamy, floating sensation.

"Do you think we could get closer?" Chloe asks

"We've just me, there's a lot we can get closer about."

"To the stage Goof-Ball!" Chloe says

"You're the driver." I say over the pounding drums. Unable to resist her over-whelming sensuality I steal a kiss.

"SNEAKY!" Chloe says as we are tightly embraced.

Everybody is swaying to the seductive, intoxicating rhythm. I feel like I'm holding the Universe in my hand, under the powerful spell that envelopes you when all of your primal senses are activated, alive, and living on the edge of your skin.

"AHHhhrrrRrRRRrR!" I roll my tongue in a
wild howl. People around me yell along, our
animated eyes meet in a mutual acknowledgement
of the raw energy that we feel. It is a fools utopia
of pure pleasure. We are submerged in a
subterranean of rhythmic madness! Stomping our
feet like a stampede of wild buffalo, our bodies
are gyrating in-between one another's and

entwined in a blurred sweet soaked Roman Orgy…

Raw electric energy is raging from the stage, then Silence!

The air that was filled a second ago with exotic melodies is now DEAD SILENT and all the lights have been cut! In the darkness we can hear each other breath. Everyone is dizzy with the echo of music rattling in our minds. The lingering buzz of silenced amplifiers is resonating in my ears.

Softly a single flute starts to sing out. The pied-piper begins to weave his cosmic notes of every color through the darkness. His melody starts faint and broken but quickly begins to take shape, taking on the shapes of ancient tales he paints the story for us to marvel at and it is becoming more colorful and intense, growing louder and louder until his heavy breath and grunts hand off his amazing solo to the crowd…

We erupt into fanatical cheers of ecstasy! All of us are moving like ocean creatures with phantom eyes, UNBELIEVABLE!

We clap and Telepathically the band picks up the rhythm of our claps of thunder, taking command of our roar and goes back into the aquatic melody of flailing butterflies, tigers, and jungle creatures...

All of us are dancing in the plasma mix of music and lights in a pagan dance of ancient stoned fascination. The music is a primal orchestra of wicked sounds, an incredible jungle of exotic bodies and mystical rivers to explore. Inside the melody you can be anyone, all your faults and transgressions are washed away and cleansed by the music. It is like being the chaotic ball on a roulette wheel, spinning you can fall into any slot. While the ball bounces you are infinite possibility, the music shatters any mold that defines you.

After 30 minutes of increasing feelings of groundless free floating the music goes into an explosive waterfall of crashing cymbals! Out of the diamond sharp eruption of cymbals the flute begins to unfold out of its cocoon of chaos. He harnesses the energy of all that just was into his single breath. We all become silent, absorbing the celestial flute. We begin to float into the Pied-Pipers tapestry of notes as he sings us the songs of the mystics, blowing his music and grunts into our ears, our minds flutter to heights our bodies cannot follow. His notes slowly fade into silence and we are enveloped once again by the empty silence and darkness!

Incredible! Like standing on the open desert watching a storm gather, then being washed by its intensity of wind, thunder, lightning, and rain... To watch the storm pass over, whisping away on the breath of the flute!

"Welcome back to the oyster shell, we have been waiting for you!" I yell.

Chloe's screaming with laughter, jumping, and clapping! If I had wings I would never come down! All things are here, just like the nitrous vision, a moment eternal clarity. The past, the future, and the present are all wound into a single breath and shared collectively with everyone here.

People won't understand, but we do we went to the oyster shell and went to see the pearl glowing.

I wrap my arms around Chloe and as if she reads my mind she jumps up, wrapping her legs around me. In the name of star-crossed lover we kiss like Gods! Locked inside a universe of musical notes representing every galaxy we are two drifting fragments of ancestral stars that have intersected orbits here in New Orleans, fused together by the music our souls have become one.

"I've never felt anything like you." Chloe says.

"This is the day I should have read my horoscope." I say.

"Then it wouldn't have happened." Chloe says.

"You can't hide from fate." I say.

"No, but you can scare it away if you are looking for it!" Chloe says.

"Wild rumpus has wrapped her fate around me!" I say.

"El composino. My crazy country boy!" Chloe says.

"Bueno loco chica!"

"Tu eres peligroso!" Chloe says.

"Only as dangerous as you let me be." I say.

"Jasper, let us drink to that."

"Chloe we are so alike it is scary."

"MMMMmmmmmmmuuUUUUuuppPPP!" She kisses me and slides down to her feet.

"Baby, baby, baby, BABY!" I chant as I split the crowd in a direct bee-line to the bar.

"What are you having." I ask.

"How about we do a shot of Rumplemintz."

"Sounds like a start, I'm going to get a Rum and coke too."

"In that case, I'll have a Pink Martini."

"Sophisticated lady!" I say.

" Yezzz I am, once you clean away all the dirt!" Chloe laughs.

Both of us are laughing as a spot opens up at the bar just big enough for me. Chloe wiggles in front of me under my arms. A hip bartender is slinging drinks from the almighty fountain of obliteration. He has a thick southern accent and asks, "Can I have your list of demands."

Chloe places our order while I breath on her neck and in her ear. He delivers our shots and starts mixing our cocktails and becomes a multi-tentacle squid.

"To the oyster shell inviting us back." I tell Chloe as I watch Tipitina's become filled with ocean creatures. The sound waves carries them like water in this state and the weightless creatures float all around me.

"To whatever may wait ahead tonight!" Chloe toasts not aware of the transformation that has taken place, or is she?

The sweet mint flavor burns all the way to my stomach and the vapor therapeutically clears my chest. I am back at the oyster shell with this mermaid named Chloe.

"MMMmmmMMmmMM!" I love this candy." Chloe says licking her lips and I see her tail rise in a shimmering blue behind her.

"You know every trick about being a mermaid." I say as my eyes are big as golf balls.

Chloe giggles, giving me a bashful look that gets her anything her pretty face desires. She tilts her head and gives me a kiss. I feel the currents pulling us together as she is moving like a belly dancer charming me...

"There are so many shortcuts that lead to extraordinary experiences and you are one!" Chloe says.

"Cheers to that." I say and we clank glasses. Chloe sips her pink martini and I drink my rum and coke. "It is cocktail hour!" I say.

"When isn't it?" Chloe asks.

"Chloe, I'm alarmed we have never met before. How long have you been hiding in the oyster shell?"

"Where are you saying? Oyster shell? Where are you staying? Do you have a place here?"

"Sure enough, would you like to join me?" I shift away from the oyster shell and regain my composure.

"I was thinking about getting off my feet."

"Lets get a cab." I say.

"I've got to let Suzy know." Chloe says.

"Let's put a note on her windshield." I say.

"what about your friends?" Chloe asks.

We both look at one another and say… 'A note on the windshield!' Laughing we flip over two coasters and write; Had to go, sexual adventure calls! After we finish our drinks we race to the door, bouncing to the chants of the Wild Magnolias. Professor Longhair smiles at us as we walk out the door of the aquatic world that is pulsing through the thick mist of this unusual night.

Once the notes are on the windshield we have no problem scoring a cab because the band is still playing and not many people are heading out. We crawl into the back of a yellow cab that feels like a submarine to me and we dip below the radar. Where is the periscope in this unit I say as the water rises up above us.

"Third Street, a block off St Charles towards Magazine." I say.

"That is one crazy mirror." Chloe says.

"My brother sent it over to me from Saudi Arabia, I could not find one here." The driver says.

"You can see everything." I say.

The rearview mirror is shaped like a convex boomerang with an arch that lets you see from one side of the cab to the other.

"That's cool, I've never seen anything like it." Chloe says.

"Thank you, the mirrors are common in Saudi Arabia."

"Was it expensive?" I ask.

"A hundred bucks."

"That was a well spent greenback."

The rear view mirror is stretching the whole cab inside its 3x12 inch world. Our faces are big in the center stretching into the rest of the cab trailing off like two alleys into the distance.

Before the amazement wears off I have to tell the driver we're here and he rises the cab from below the water.

"That'll be $5.65 please." The driver says.

"Keep the change." I hand the driver a ten. Chloe and I hop out of the cab and water spills out of the doors. I realize that I am tripping as he peels off.

"Chloe, sweet Chloe" I say.

"Yes Jasper, my train wreck Jasper. Look at those saucers!" She says giggling.

I look up and ask, "do you see a UFO?"

"Those eyes!" She points to me.

"Tonight is a night of crazy love! We leave our inhibitions on this side of the gate." I say.

"I already left mine at the airport!" Chloe says.

"Where are you from?" I ask.

"Tonight your dreams COWBOY!" Chloe says.

She is from the oyster shell I think..?

With the gate closed behind us and Chloe's hand in mine, wide eyed and glowing we float down the sidewalk. As we step into the courtyard Chloe says; "This is amazing! The waterfall is beautiful. Jasper this place is incredible!"

As Chloe flies around the courtyard like a hummingbird in an exotic flower garden I throw open the French doors and crank up some Rolling Stones and pull the bed out of the couch.

"Welcome to my Buddhist den of cosmic Chaos! Welcome!"

"I love it; the yard smells like a giant honeysuckle." Chloe says.

"You're a true cosmic child. Do you know what cosmic means?"

"Tell me."

"The definition I read and like the most is; so pervasive and all inclusive as to exist in or affect the whole world. You are cosmic Chloe."

"Yeah that's me. Do you have any Van Morrison?"

"Sure do, which album?"

"Philosopher Stone, Ordinary People."

"Good choice, that is exactly how I feel to quote Van the man Morrison" "I fell things that ordinary people just can't comprehend."

"Jasper can I light these candles?"

"Go ahead, candles are meant to burn, shine bright, and not collect dust."

"Candles are like a humans mind because they stay dark until they are lit by ambition and inspired with ideas."

"Deep, our minds can go dark, then BAM! Be caught a blaze by another persons spark."

"Exactly, we are all like that. We become settled from routine life."

"Chloe you're a mix of timeless harmony and beautiful imagination you're a MIRICLE HYBRID!"

"This place feels like a country ranch."

"New Orleans is the biggest small town I've ever been to." I say as I wrap my arms around Chloe. We fall back into the pile of blankets on the bed. Van Morrison's singing and fire dances on the candles and through our kisses.

We are nose to nose, fingers to fingers, lying in bed smelling each others scent. My heart is beating fast. The feeling is so strong that every door in my body, spirit and mind is open. A rush of emotions are inviting Chloe into me.

"Chloe you're my new obsession." I whisper lightly into her ear.

"I didn't expect to come to Mardi Gras and find someone like you."

"There is nothing like your touch in my memory. I do not feel human, this is beyond mortal." I say.

A thick moist air is between our faces as we share each others breath. Fingers to fingers, rolling our hands' together like two tiger tails intertwined in the darkness, light reflecting in our eyes; "Take my hand of light" she says to me without using her voice.

On the wings of dreams Chloe lifts us up into a cosmic spiral lined with millions of doors. From here we can walk into any world, all possibilities or we can stay here in this warm nebula of love, golden laughter, and carefree abandon… Here, inside this spiral super nova galaxy of light.

I am in her embrace, the embrace of reckless abandon… On a journey that will test me until I break and shatter into infinity! No self, no ego, no care... Free beyond the resistance of care, happily embracing the butterfly, learning clumsily how to take to the wind. On wings of silver, bouncing gently on the warm breeze until a chill comes calling us into the comfort of a flower.

There we strip to the very essence of all that we are. We wrap the flower around us, enveloped, so soft, so beautiful Chloe is... Glowing, a world opens up to us of glistening blue water rushing over our skin. Cascading over a waterfall, the water dissolves us, we vanish and become liquid!

Our bodies are drops of water. We touch, rolling over one another, playing, making incredible connection we take shape to embrace and kiss. The passion becomes uncontainable... we burst into liquid! Rising and falling in the loud cascading water my body shifts from air to mist and then water drops. Weightless I rise and fall!

Chloe becomes the rainbow glow of mist. I laugh and send ripples through her colors then she wraps around me. We fall to the river making love. Tumbling down the river mercy has found me! Mercy has found me and given me the love of the universe, the miracle of infinite love! We're wrapped in a blanket of light as we wash up on the shore like a skipping stone from the glowing blue water onto the whitest sandy shore.

Totally immersed in each other sharing the love that only reckless abandon knows, we are wrapped in the mist of creation.

Softly we roll along the sand and we roll between the covers of a fairytale. Our bodies morph into words and we become made up of letters... A breeze blows the book open and Chloe jumps out. I follow her letter laced silhouette. Her body is a jumble of letters with light pouring through all the spaces in-between. We run around in circles, reaching out, touching each others arms…

In our connection we make every word, every thought, and lightening pours out of our connection as we touch! We are caught in a zone between worlds, made up of fantasy, laced in letters…

Chloe's eyelids become two butterflies. They flutter around off her face, floating around and above us. We laugh and kiss as sentences pour from our beings, the words they form come to life and creation surrounds us. We are at the epicenter of fascination, a fascination so profound that fills us with a sense of wonder and awe as we shudder back into our flesh!!!

Chloe is a golden beauty! Sunshine pours from her lips…

"I love you! She says… "I love you too!" I say.

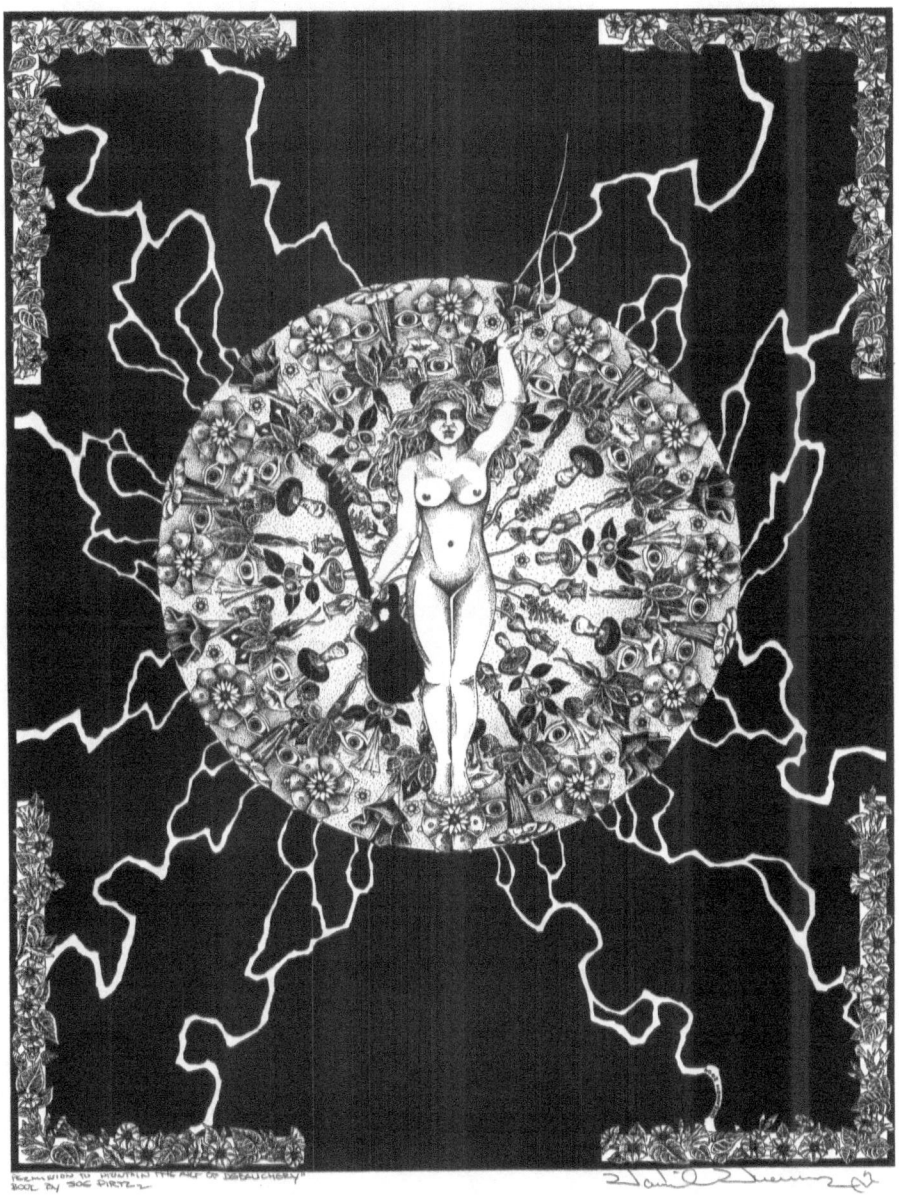

Naked with my head on Chloe's belly I wake up. Softly I lick her nipple with the tip of my tongue. I love her scent and the salty taste of her skin. She's still dreaming so I lift myself as quietly out of bed as I can.

Mother of god, I've slept through another New Orleans morning, it is already 12:30! The morning is gone but the night was pure magic! I've got my Cinderella wrapped up in dreams on my bed. Infinite happiness sweeps over me as I look at Chloe the biggest smile of my life forms on my lips… I have fell asleep with Chloe and woke up in a fantasy!

This moment calls for a Peruvian group of traditional instruments called 'Inca Samia.' It is soothing, floating music that takes all the edges away. Next mission is fruit smoothies. There's nothing like a fresh fruit smoothie when you wake up!

I pull the ice box open and get to work and a blast of thick white frozen air slowly reveals the frozen fruit. Frozen banana's blueberries and strawberries are key to good smoothies, I don't use ice. By using the frozen fruit the smoothie stays thick and not watered down like an ice smoothie does. I throw handfulls of each fruit into my jumbo blender, top it with a heap of vanilla organic yogurt, a splash of milk and smother it in golden honey. After the mounds of each are added I slap the lid on and push the button.

The blender growls like a washing machine loaded with gravel, vicious! The noise is going to wake Chloe, so I decide to do it myself with a warm kiss of honey soaked lips.

Lips to lips I can barely resist laughing. Chloe moans as she slowly comes to life. Her mouth is flooding with flavor.

"Yummy, my crazy honey bee."

"Hear that?"

"Yeah, is that the angry hive?"

"Fruit smoothies, the best in town!"

"Awesome, I've got to tinkle."

"My house is your house."

"My body is yours…" Chloe giggles and we both laugh. Chloe puts her finger on my nose and says; "BIM SHAKAH BOOM!" as she gets up. Her nakid body flawlessly floats across the room I HOOOOOWWWWLLLLLL at her full moon ass!

Chloe finds me in the courtyard sitting at the table wearing my thick framed sunglasses. With a note pad and a pen in my hand I am madly scribbling away.

"Hey baby, what are you writing?"

"About life, you, this and the things that happen between the breath of life. I'm trying to capture the raw essence of life that we experience in the path of reckless abandon refining our art, the art of debauchery."

"MMmmm, sounds as yummy as this delicious fruit smoothie. We could get rich selling these."

I look up, Chloe's wearing a white tank top barely covering her nipples. I ask her; "Have you ever seen those little flashing lights?"

"Maybe, you have to be more specific than that. In the sky, Neon?"

"They have magnets on the back and people wear them on their clothes, their ears, anywhere."

"You mean blinkies?"

"Exactly, blinkies! I've got three cases of them and that my dear is how we are going to get rich!"

"Brilliant, sounds smashing. Marvelous darling!"

"Yeah, I paid .50 cents for each one and we sell them for $5 bucks."

"Damn, that's pure profit. My kind of gig."

"Tonight, we're going to start off at the Dragon's den."

"I love the Dragon's Den. It's a turn of the century opium den that's survived the decades in decadence. The Dragon's den is still the same pot smoking dark spot reserved for those who are in the know. Brain freeze never tasted so good." We laugh and sip our smoothies. The afternoon is warm and lovely and the smell of magnolias fills the air.

Pointing at a squid shaped hand held glass bubbler I say… "That has a fresh 'John Glen' bud with your name written all over it."

"I've never heard of John Glen bud before."

"It's a Grape Afghani crossed with Meigs County golden that I created. I call it John Glenn because it gets you as high as the first man who walked on the moon!" I say as Chloe looks at the bowl.

"These metallic colors are groovy."

"It's fresh and your hit, batter up!"

Chloes eyes are like pools of tropical green lakes translucent in the sun. She is wide eyed and eager, I flick the bick and say "ENJOY!"

Chloe's cross eyed as she stares down the end of her nose watching the bubbler fill up with smoke. The weed starts to blaze, her mouth is round and her cheeks are dimpled. She looks like a fish with wide glowing eyes. The smoke is curling out of the bowl and a thick smoke is filling her lungs. I don't think she realizes what she is in for, she is puffing hard!

"That's a girl, you're a trooper!"

"AAAHhh!" Chloe lets out as she pulls the bubbler from her juicy lips and sets it into my hands.

"You look like a balloon." No sooner do I say this that Chloe explodes, hacking violently! She gets up and jumps around like a fool! The only thing I can do is laugh! The air fills with the dank smell of potent home-grown pot! Chloe looks like she inhaled the poison apple. She becomes a dancing dragon spitting smoke from her lungs. After her wild flailing she hangs her head down, puts her hands on her knees and catches her breath. She flings her head back and tears are rolling around her smiling cheeks! Blood shot eyes and a cherry bomb face with THC firing through her lava veins.

"You look like hell." I say.

"One hit wonder!" Chloe mutters.

"I wondered, when is Chloe going to slow down? TOO LATE!"

"This John Glen shoots through you! It is sooo grapey and lands you on the moon!"

"You just shook your own rug Miss Iron Lung." I say as I start to take a toke. The John Glen is like syrup into my lungs of sweet grape crystal dreams. On the edge of the euphoric lake I dive in and inhale!

"Come on dreamer, take a bigger hit than that and dream!"

I shake my head -NO- and clear the smoke out of the bubbler, then set it down. I lean my head back, blowing smoke rings I watch them twist and rise into the air, they are dark and stay visible until I have five smoke rings floating in the air. Chloe stands on her chair and puts her finger through them. The turbulence makes the rings ripple like oil spots warping into a new dimension.

"How do you feel?" I ask.

"Fabulous darling everything is groovy and I am terribly relaxed!"

"Would you rub my neck for me? I have a kink in it from sleeping with my head on your belly, so we could say its your fault!"

"HA, you dirty rat! I'll rub your neck just after I have a sip of my smoothie."

She brings her icy fingers to my neck. "This is love!" I mutter over my moans of pleasure.

"You haven't felt anything yet!" Chloe says as her fingers start to melt me. I feel like a bowl of jello. She works up my neck to my ear, E-GADS! I am liquid lava! Chloe is massaging my ear with her thumb on the back side of my ear and her index finger is slowly rolling through the curves of the front side of my ear.

"Liquid Lava!" I moan as Chloe breathes warmly into my ear which turns my skin into vapor as Chloe rolls my ear into a ball. My skin becomes a billion tingles of cold fire. My eyelids feel heavy and my brain has a fuzzy sensation washing all over my frontal lobes. I flip my head back and Chloe's lips meet mine lighting up my 2 million chakras exposing a fascinating world of sensory colors. I reach up to Chloe's etheric body and put my hand on the back of her head. We begin nibbling on each others lips. Her hand is still tracing my ear.

"Jasper, I see you've made friends." Comes from outside of my head. My neurotransmitters are sparking off and someone is interrupting my fantasy… "Jasper come up for air!"

"Fuck off!" I mumble and Chloe breaks off to great who-ever is here.

"Yeah Moss, why now?"

"I'm going to whole foods, thought you might want to go."

"Calm down, graduate to a smoothie, smoke some weed… You remember Chloe?"

"Nice to see you again in the light of day."

"You too Moss, beautiful day." Chloe says tugging on her loose tank top that is exposing her bare breast.

"I wondered what happened to you last night." Moss says giving us a big grin.

"Now you see." Chloe says with a smile.

"There is still a lot left to the imagination! About that I will always wonder, but to change the subject some of the coolest people you ever meet on day just up and vanish. Out of no where they come and then vaporize! Leaving you to wonder, where the fuck did they go?"

"And?" I ask.

"And you find out they have been busted! Looking at 10 years for a drug possession charge for being at a house during a raid, or at a house with a lab."

"Moss is this someone you know?"

"Yeah, I met this girl, one of the coolest chicks

you'll ever meet. I met her and after two weeks she asks me to watch her house and feed her cats for the weekend and that she will be back in four days. I volunteer and on the eight day with no sign of her I began to worry, I decided to answer the phone and it was her mother, her mom asked me to watch the house until she gets down here in a week or two. Turns out she was at a heroin house that had four kilos of Girl and now she's looking at between 8 to 15 years." Moss says.

"Damn, that's crazy!" Chloe says.

"I know, she was going to Tulane and getting good grades. Her place was nice, nice furniture, an expensive stereo, and great art on the walls so I wondered. She was one of the coolest girls I'll ever meet, GONE, vanished into the void!"

"Another victim of the 'DRUG WAR." Chloe says.

"From sugar to shit!" I say.

"If this is a war we need to be more organized. The law is ruining lives, it needs to be ruining lives on both sides!" Moss says.

"Man, they have the Judges, the Prosecutors, the courtrooms, the bailiffs, and the media ALL ON THEIR SIDE. They are even allowed to break the law! THE SYSTEM IS RIGGED WITH CORRUPTION!" I say.

"I believe it all goes back to prohibition, they figured out how to make money and keep society confused, along with filling jails and stripping our civil rights!" Chloe says.

"The auto industries are gone, the steel mills are gone, the shipyards are gone, and the manufacturing jobs are all in CHINA! The only large scale industry left is in law enforcement and dealing drugs. You drive down any street in anywhere America and it is lined with crack houses in some part of it! The most remote towns are infected and Washington D.C. is in terminal stages of sickness!" I say.

"The system is so bad here in 'Free America' that soon we are going to have multi-generational incarceration. Children locked up with parents and grandparents locked up with their grandchildren." Chloe says.

"The prison population is the driving force in stabilizing the economy, all those people are out of the job market." Moss Says.

"Bullshit laws with no end! And, everyone is to scared to speak out, afraid of the system. Academic professors do not speak their minds, they go by an unsigned agreement that they will support the system even when they know otherwise and that is a root of all this!" Chloe says.

"Just throw it on." I say.

"What?" Chloe asks.

"Reggea, Moss is plugged into the rasta vibe." I say.

"I be in luv wit da rasta philosophy, mon! I raise my glass to all the fallen brothers and sisters who are sitting in the belly of the beast!" Moss toasts.

"Cheers, cheers, cheers…" We clank our glasses and finish off the smoothies, they are sooooooo delicious!

"Who are you throwing in, Bob Marely?" Chloe asks.

"Burning Spear, or Carl Dawkins." Moss answers from inside the living room.

"Marijuana is called yerva in espanol." Chloe says.

"Si, mi gusta la moto muy mucho!" I say.

"Build your penitentiaries, we build your schools, brainwash education, then you make us the fools… Gonna chase these crazy, chase those crazy bullies OUTTA TOWN!" Bob Marely sings…

"Chloe do you know about Jack Herer?" I ask.

"Sounds familiar, why do I know that name?"

"He's the man behind California's Medical Marijuana Initive. He also gathered every document ever printed about Hemp and Marijuana in a book called 'The Emperor Wears no Clothes' that is incredible."

"What all did you learn?"

"The gateway drug –Marijuana- was made illegal on a Friday night at 5:45 P.M. and the debate lasted under TWO MINUTES! TWO MINUTES, THREE QUESTIONS, AND NOW POT IS THE BACKBONE OF THE 'WAR ON DRUGS!" I proclaim.

"We've been BAMBOOZLED!" Chloe says.

"Exactly! BAMBOOZLED! BY OUR OWN GOVERNMENT!" I say.

"We're wiping our asses with trees! Each acre of hemp grows in one season and produces the same amount of paper as 4 acres of trees THAT TAKE 30 YEARS TO GROW! And hemp doesn't require the chemicals that trees do to break down their fibres." Moss chimes in.

"What do you boys know about nuclear power?" Chloe asks.

"That the waste lasts for-ever, FOR-EVER!" Moss says.

"Just about. The plutonium is so hot that it stays suspended in flush pools of fresh water that circulates through the holding tank and back into the river. Get this, the water is no longer water, the molecular structure has become altered to hydrogen and damages the river life." Chloe says.

"That is fucked up!" I say.

In the background Bob Marley is wailing away at his last concert he performed while alive, it was at the Stanley Theatre, Pittsburgh Pa Sept 23, 1980. of all places. The show has an Ire vibe with mad energy to the sound.

"After ten years in the cooling pools the spent waste is then moved into the next stage; It is encased in steel cylinders that will be encased in thick cement where it has to remain for the next 200,000 years! At last the radio active levels will be broken down enough to be non-toxic." Chloe says.

"200,000 years? God have mercy on our ignorant souls, mankind is making a floating coffin for our legacy to our children!" Moss says.

"Really, show me something that man has made that lasts for 5,000 years intact, let alone 200,000 years." I say.

"LET'S START A MOVEMENT, AN EVOLUTION! REVOLUTIONS REVOLVE, WE HAVE TO EVOLVE!" Chloe says and sparks the bubbler.

"The COURT SYSTEM IS BROKEN, JUSTICE IS BEING SLAUGHTERED! WE NEED TO MOVE OUR NUMBERS TO THE STREETS AND HOLD COURT IN THE STREETS!" I rail off in an animated spirit.

"Medicine that cures disease and costs so much have ALL been paid for by TAX PAYERS DOLLARS then as soon as a medicine is approved the company who developed the meds with the peoples money applies for a patent number at the patent office. Once the patent is issued the medicine that the AMERICAN TAX DOLLARS PAID FOR BELONGS TO THE PHARMACUTICAL GIANT who will reap HUGE profits instead of distributing the cure to the sick who paid to develop the cure! American's are robbed by the grace of congress of the cures that rightfully belongs to every American, ROBBED!" Moss says.

"BAMBOOZLED, WE'VE BEEN BAMBOOZLED!" Chloe shouts.

"Work hard to starve." Moss says.

"ENJOYMENT – NOT - EMPLOYEMENT!" I SAY.

"Our leaders have sold us out! Truth is deception in the American political system, and politicians! Washington D.C. stole and sold the United States middles class to sweat shops around the globe." Moss says.

"Uncle Sam extends the hand of poverty to all Americans! A suicidal elected body drums the war beat with the bones of our ancestors. EVERY ELECTED OFFICIAL KNOWS THAT THEIR POSITION IS TEMPORARY AND CONTINUES WITH THE FEVERISH CLIMATE OF TERMINAL POLICY MAKING THAT INFECTS WASHINGTON D.C… FATAL POLICIES ARE BEING CREATED BY

POLITICAINS WHO DISCOUNT AMERICA TO A 'ONE TERM ONLY' MENTALITY! The retched policies are inherited by the next elected official who, like the Greek mythological snake the Oroboros that perpetually eats itself carries out the business of dismantling the American dream. Suicidal policy makers with the terminal term disease are vaporizing America!" Chloe says.

"Our heads, full of radical ideas. Do you have the nerve to do something about it?" I ask.

"I'm not doing anything after Mardi Gras, at least for a day." Chloe reads my eyes laughing.

"Hell yes! I'm aboard with you fireball. We will take one day off then start the evolution." I say.

"Its not good enough that I know, that my neighbor knows, that our parents know! We know that D.C. knows that we know, we have to take defense to the criminals that have no

opposition; THE GOVERNMENT ITSELF!"
Chloe says.

"Mother of the revo- I MEAN EVOLUTION!"
I say.

"Right on, sounds sexy." Moss says.

"Laws have been people managers since the first government. A guise for maintaining wealth and property lines through manipulation and fear of the population." I say.

"Every right we have has been paid for in precious blood to those brave and defiant enough to stand and fight." Chloe says.

"The pig has enforced and preserved the law with his blackjack on the skulls of righteous Americans with the blessings of Congress. We have to be smart." Moss says.

"Even bullets! The Kent State Massacre, we can't forget those who fell dead on the other side of the very National Guard's riffles who we're sworn to protect Americans. And in the Appalachian mountains congress approved the only bombing campaign ever on American citizens who were on strike at the coal mines!" I say.

"We have all acknowledged these heinous acts and NOW, TODAY! We pledge part of our energy to stand as a movement! Our bond has tightened and a stoned pact has been made. I read somewhere once that the mind once stretched by a new idea can no longer go back to it's original shape." Chloe Says.

"I SUMMON THE WARRIOR SPIRIT TO PUT THE FIGHT IN OUR HEARTS, WISDOM IN OUR MINDS, ENDURANCE IN OUR BREATH, AND NUMBERS AT OUR SIDES! MAY WE RISE STRONG, DETERMINED, AND TRIUMPH!" I say.

"A VOICE OF TRUTH CANNOT BE SILENCED WHEN MANY TONGUES SPEAK TOGETHER." Moss says.

"I love that Moss, great line!" I say.

"BLESSED ARE THOSE WHO HUNGER AND THIRST FOR RIGHTESNES, FOR THEY SHALL BE FILLED. BLESSED ARE THOSE WHO ARE PERSECUTED FOR RIGHTEOUSNESS' SAKE, FOR THEIRS IS THE KINGDOM OF HEAVEN! BLESSED ARE YOU, WHEN THEY REVILE AND PERSECUTE YOU AND SAY ALL KINDS OF EVIL AGAINST YOU FALSELY FOR MY SAKE, REJOICE FOR SO THEY PERSECUTED THE PROPHETS BEFORE YOU!" Chloe quotes Mathew.

"Where'd you get that from?" Moss asks.

"Sermon on the mountain, gospel 5-10, my father is a preacher." Chloe says with a smile of southern pride.

We are enjoying the sunny afternoon puffing herb, animated, and listening to Bob Marley. LIFE IS GOOD! We are pioneers, trail blazers, engaged in the continual evolution! The first genuine confirmation is living what you believe in. You have to and that I am!

"Pot is a peace maker by its very nature. It brings you into a circle close together to pass the pipe around." Moss says.

"Junkies hold the weight of the world on their shoulders and suffer the pain of humanity." Chloe says.

"All for the greater cause than our individual selves, out of the radical chaos will some will rise to be the greatest artists, philosophers, scientists, thinkers, musicians, doctors, leaders, poets, and muses the world will ever have known. Being slandered by the system, locked up in jail, and put through hardships until one rises up in defiance through the net. When they rise to do so bringing many with them and their courage is passed from one to another until the movement unifies humanity!" Moss says.

"Yeah, the system that breaks down the spirit embraces the person once they have overcome all the trails. Then they absorb that individual into their system, kind of makes a corporation out of the person and regurgitates the message in their form. Cultural assimilation!

"Only as long as the public demands that the Rights which so hard a fight was fought to gain not be revoked... Then will we keep these rights. As soon as you blink the government steels our freedoms back from us though because the government has unlimited man power, money, and time to dismantle any movement." Chloe says.

"Truth is deception in the American Politician. Industrial, pharmaceutical, and oil lobbies control the senate. The money flows where the money flows!" Moss says.

"Look at how the 'War on Drugs' is being fought by the same dope dealer who is pushing manufactured drugs on children and building a dependent nature at a young age which will lead them through a life of addiction. At a young age the Doctors are diagnosing kids for attention disorders, hyper-active syndrome, natural energies of being a kid and prescribing the answer in a pill bottle- It is WRONG!" Chloe says.

"It makes sense to the Devil." Moss says.

Lifting my head from my note book as I capture the conversation I ask "What day is it?"

"Thursday." Moss answers.

"I have to visit the swamp tomorrow; I have a date with the Mojo Man."

"For what?" Chloe asks.

"A big Mardi Gras surprise, that is all I am going to tell you."

"OH-SHIT!" Moss says laughing, then asks us if we are ready to go to Whole Foods.

"I better call my friends before they get worried about me."

"The phone is next to the bed."

"I've been calling all morning and getting a busy signal." Moss says.

"We have been busy!"

As Chloe is in talking to her friends Moss raves over how hot Chloe is. Chloe is one red hot mama.

"What did you get into last night?"

"The music went till 5 A.M. and then I staggered out of Tips and headed to Snakey Jakes. I was fucked up."

"A true drunken fiend on the rollercoaster waves of New Orleans."

"It's Mardi Gras with hotties everywhere you eyeballs land, and they are drunk, high, and

Horney! We walk into Jakes and at the back corner booth is Fly, I blink my disbelieving eyes and no, it's not my imagination, Fly is fucking his girlfriend right there!"

"There must have been some mojo in the air last night because Chloe and I did the same thing between the streets outside of Tips high on a nitrous buzz last night." I say as Moss's mouth is gaping with wide eyes looking around me at Chloe in the living room.

"Her body isn't the only dynamite; she is a radical minded diva!" Moss says.

"Poster girl of the evolution." I say.

319

Looking at Chloe I feel a sense of pride. Now that last nights dust is settled I have a moment of clarity, the calm before the storm and feel comforted knowing I have Chloe to inspire me on the ride. She is sitting cross legged Indian style, our eyes are locked in on each others, and she blows me a kiss and smiles.

"Hey Jasper my friends are dying to meet you."

"We'll be at Whole Foods in a half an hour."

"All right we will rendezvous there."

Mardi Gras sometime in the vortex...

Carpe Diem!

Get your third eye painted by this

Jolly fellow!

Art of clowning around!

"Sounds good." I get up with the bubbler and head into the bunker. Everything is a mess and night is still clinging to the clutter. The candles have splattered wax onto the floor and the bed is a wreck. I walk into the bathroom and start brushing my teeth, looking into my eyes watching them dilate, organically shifting from green to blue as the pupil dilates altering the pattern. In

the black I can see my whole body reflecting
inside my eye.

Brilliant in Color like it will be this year!

For sure he has a big smile crawlen
through the thick of Pardi Gras!

My buddy Will Roth out of the Blue!

www.suzannesaundersartwork.com

for the greatest face paintings! and art too!

Strange, I wonder, when your eye dilates, where does the color go? It is still there, but it pushes to the outside of the orb when the black gets bigger and then expands when the pupil shrink. I am thinking of the ocean waves I saw in Chloe's eyes, circling her pupils and then the expanse of infinite space opened inside of her center of her eyes. I saw a universe expand...

"What are you doing?" Chloe sneeks into the bathroom to find me inches away from the mirror in some trance state.

 "Wondering where the color goes when our eyes dilate."

Chloe throws here back against the wall laughing at me. I spin around pinning Chloe with my arms and elbows. My lips to Chloe's giggling mouth and our eyes are wide open as we kiss with our mouths vibrating from laughter and hot breath. "I need five minutes in here alone." Chloe says.

 "The bathroom is all yours." I move outside the bathroom as Chloe closes the door down to my single eye, then SHUT! I would do a split if only I could like James Brown growlen 'I FEEL GOOD' because Chloe is my new found obsession.

"FREAK BOY let your freak flag fly!" Moss says.

"I wear it in the sparkle of my eyes."

"Are you two ready to go?"

"Soon as Chloe comes out."

"BOO!" Chloe shakes me.

"That didn't scare me but your nails digging into my side sure feels good."

I lock the doors and we heard to the street. Moss is driving his toy-O-ta pick up truck. Along the dashboard are furry chunks of Jasper, strange nuts, crystals, natural wonders, and other souvenirs from road trips zig-zagging the American highways. We pile in with Chloe in the middle and andiamos! We are off.

Flying down 3rd street to Magazine Street Mardi Gras pepper the sidewalk. People are sitting outside the restaurants with mountains of beer piled on the tables and the day is only beginning. We pull as close to Whole Foods as we can and exit the truck to join in the busy rush of people who flow in and out of the market. Before we hit the doo one of Chloe's friends signals us down and we walk over to her. She is cute and dressed in tight hip huggers with a short shirt exposing her belly button that has a pierce inside it.

"Andrea-OH MY GOD-WHAT A CRAZZZZYYYY NIGHT! You met Jasper last night, this is Moss. Moss, Andrea, Andrea, Moss." Chloe says.

"Nice to meet you Andrea."

"You too Moss, how the hell are you Jasper?"

"Marvelous! Chloe is a star child."

"I hope I didn't have you worried this morning." Chloe tells Andrea.

"It takes more than one night to worry me. Ron and Terry are already in the store shopping, shall we?"

We grab a buggy and enter the market. Whole foods is an all organic grocery store with grain raised beef, and open range raised chicken and burgers from cattle that has no antibiotic or growth hormones tastes better than a steak from the industrial ranches that mass produce meat. First stop is the beer isle which is 30 foot of micro-brews! A heavenly wonder for my thirst! I pick up two six packs, one is 'Tommy Knocker's Maple Nut' and the other is my favorite; Sierra Nevada Pale ale. Chloe gets a four pack of Sammy Smith, Moss grabs a six pack of 'Flyen Dog' and Andrea is in awe over the selection. She finally gets a couple bottles of grape lambeck that cost a cool eight dollars each.

We throw some snack foods in for good measure, blue chips, salsa, hummus, avocados, and a couple of lemons to make guacamole. We gather enough food to reach an agreement that it will fill us up and we head for the registers. Leaving the store we find Terry and Ron eating sushi wraps at a table and Terry says to Chloe, "Well, if it isn't the mystery girl herself, the great Houdini."

They have a huge platter of sushi wraps and we all dig in and devour them over a rhythmic rant of conversation. The mound of wasabi lights you up, it is like heat that soaks into your every pore and opens you wide up. Wasabi is a truly unique experience of horse powered spice.

Ron's place is just down the road and he invites us to go smoke a South American plant called Salvia spiked with DMT. Salvia has a strong hallucinatory effect and the presence of a female goddess. It is an ancient herb that has been used by the natives for guidance through the spiritual world and we are not sure DMT is added to this homemade tincture or not but that is the word.

"We are off to smoke some salvia! We're off to smoke some salvia!" Moss is chanting. I'm excited too and now we are in a caravan to Ron's apartment. Chloe is riding with them so Moss and I have the chance to talk. I tell him about my night of killer sex.

"How many girls is that now?"

"Let's see, if you count the girl at the restaurant Chloe makes the third."

"Oh shit! Number three."

"What about you, Any hook up last night?"

"I'm waiting on my ex, she's coming into town on Saturday. If her an I don't hook up then it is on."

"Saturday is an eternity away."

"So is your mind you twisted fuck."

"I may be all of that and more but I don't try to deny it either."

"No you don't, that's why I love, your contagious like a virus!"

"So are you." I say.

Ron's pointing at a parking spot so we whip into the horizontal spot and jump out of the truck. Chloe runs and jumps up wrapping her thin strong legs around me she puts her hands on the sides of my face and we kiss. We kiss like reunited star struck lovers. The peanut throws in some rumbling and we notice the moans come from beyond our sphere but Chloe's heart beat is all I hear pulsing through the ether, ethereal waves rippling around us we rise.

"Are you coming?" Andrea yells, catching our attention. She's holding the door open and we run up the steps after her.

"Have a cow." Chloe says.

"MOOOOOooOO!" I sound and we laugh.

We run in the pad and tapestries and music posters line the walls. Jimi Hendrix is doing some solo blues on the stereo and the vibe cradles me, caresses me. This looks to be a promising experience!

Everyone pulls up a seat around the table, the Jimi Hendrix slides into 'Roadhouse blues' by the Doors." I feel my pulse quicken with anticipation of the high.

"The salvia is an extremely sensual presence, you may get scared. The buzz casts a heavy spell between five to ten minutes and you will be completely in her world. This is an extract and is highly concentrated, so it is very potent and it

may have DMT on it. You wont need very much.
Take a small amount at first, so you can learn
about the world your about to enter.   Jasper since
your so eager I am going to start you off on the
ride first." Ron says.

"Alright."

"Here's the way to use this contraption. I
would take one big hit, then two small hits. I'll
light it all you have to do is smoke. Take the key,
its time to open some doors!"

I'm holding a scientific flask in my hands, it is
a combination of stuff that Ron created. We all
have wide eyes, Ron flicks the butane lighter, I
exhale and take a huge rasta hit. I exhale the thick
smoke and beyond Ron's advice I take two more
Rasta tokes and cash out the bowl that was filled
for two.

My body heats up and I feel like I start boiling, my heart is beating fast, real fast, the beat of my heart starts getting loud, echoing off the walls…

The air looks like a checker board with squares piling over everything. Everyone around the table becomes one giant body in front of me, A LOOMING TERRORIZING PRESENCE! I throw my arms up and the checkers go flying, turning into a spider wed, a thick clinging spider wed pulling me into this creature!

"Spider, get the fuck away from me!" I tear the spider web off my body and turn in slow motion the horizon melts into a wall, I smack my head off the wall and start mumbling to talk myself through my confusion. The spider web starts breaking down, my body is covered in sweet and as fast as the trip came on its fading. Voices are becoming audible, Chloe is in front of me as I open my eyes. The spider web is gone and the bodies have split into their individual selves from the huge multi headed creature.

Chloe's running her hands over my body and blowing on my neck. "Give us some space." I hear her tell everyone.

My body is hot and my head feels like a brown paper bag that somebody popped. The room is still spinning and Chloe lifts my head from the spiral and cradles my head in the fold of her butterfly wings. She puts her face above mine and her hair surrounds our faces with a jet black curtain of privacy. Her liquid green-blue eyes starring into mine she welcomes me back. "Are you better?"

"That was so scary, I thought something awful of that hallucination like I was trapped in this other dimension." The fucking judge crawls back into my head "GUILTY GUILTY!" from the hotel dream but this time I am laughing as I am surrounded by the underground.

"Shush" Chloe whispers, sending a calming wave over me.

The salvia has lost its grip, the head throb is gone. After what I have just witnessed a part of me will never be the same. Chloe kisses me softly, the warmth of her lips gives a loss of words. When we release one another I do a body shake and laugh.

"What was that all about? You weird mother of freakiness?" Moss asks.

"I don't want to talk about it, I need fresh air."

"You want to go for a walk?" Chloe asks.

"Yes I would, anyone else?"

"I'm cool sitting right here." Moss says.

"You may just take off where I left off on that journey, don't let it grad hold of your soul."

"No worries my man."

"See you guys after a while." Chloe and I run down the steps. We make a stop at the truck and pour some beers into cups. "The Tommy knockers is brewed with real maple syrup and is so fucking good." I say.

"Mmmmm, that is delicious!" Chloe says licking her lips.

I tell Chloe about my experience and she tells me how crazy it was. We're walking down the sidewalk that bends with the roots of these old trees up and down. We are holding hands, smiling and feeling good about life. Everything that was shook up in my mind has fallen back into my strange sense of balance.

The streets are alive under the blue mid-day sky with white puffy clouds playing above our heads. The trees keep their leaves all year and their old arms hold the arms of the trees on the other side of the street. As we walk under the canapy I realize that we are near my maddened painter friends house and decide to stop in. Somehow our topic slides onto pills and I pull from my pocket a collection of percocets and somas Chloe grabs two of each. I eat three percocets and three somas. I swallow the somas that make me cringe with their most god awful flavor I have ever tasted, the percocets are different. I chew the percocets into an opiate milkshake and wash them down with a smile of cold beer.

"When you start to sink, hold onto me. I'll keep you up, me strong like bull." Chloe jokes flaring her nostrils and crunching her cute face.

The somas make any high a dangerous combination. They turn your body into elastic tilted world. I have stumbled sideways looking in a straight direction unable to walk the straight line to my destination.

My friends are Eric B. and Suzan Saunders. Both talented abstract artists. Eric's bike is leaning outside his house and the painted in every color storm doors are open. "Eric, Suzan! This is the police! Put the brush down and come out with the canvas up!

"Fools, you don't understand us, Jasper man, what's going on?"

"JASPER!" Suzan yells through her Cheshire cat smile inside her vortex.

"Suzan, hey its sure good to see you." We hug each other and Suzan asks; "Did you bring some of that good weed?"

"Does a frog have a water tight ass?" I reach into my pocket and pull out a small baggy of homegrown and give it to her. "This is for you."

"Well, we have to smoke some. Eric, who's your new friend?"

"Oh- this is Chloe." Eric grins mischievously, his one eye is brownish red and the other is splotched with a crazy aqua-green patch. The holograph like colors of his eyes gives him a constant shifting look. He and Suzan met at art school and moved to New Orleans to introduce their talent to the world.

"Hi Chloe, I'm Suzan, it's nice to meet you."

"Did you do all the artwork?"

"This is just a little of our work. We have a studio in the warehouse district too."

The whole first room of their house is covered, every square inch from the floor to the ten foot high ceilings is COVERED in paintings. Paintings on the tops of tables, paintings on the top of bookshelves, on the top of their couches, paintings on top of paintings! THE ROOM IS DRIPPING LIKE AN ABSTRACT OASIS OF MIRRORS!

"You know the best part of being an artist?" Chloe asks Suzan.

"Your creative?" Suzan answers.

"That too, but you get to have so much amazing artwork."

"True."

Eric takes Chloe to show her around and a spinning sound grabs hold of my attention. It's a toy from my child hood days that is the size of a lunchbox with a button on the top. When you push the button three rows of squares spin and in each row is three squares that used to have different people who get mixed up in the spin. Eric has painted crazy bodies that are hilarious when they stack up. This is the coolest thing I have seen all day!

"I love it!" Chloe pushes the button, when the piece finally stops spinning we all bust into a riot of laughter.

"Everything in this room is for sale except this, and Suzan."

I ask if that is true and wrap my arm around Suzan.

"Wow, your eyes are cool! Do you see differently out of that one that is half brown and half green?" Chloe asks Eric.

"No but everybody is mesmerized by my eyes."

"I brought some acid down here." I say.

"I bet you did. How's Mardi Gras treating you?" Suzan asks.

"Your looking at Chloe, she's part of the answer! It has been sleepless, drunken, and musically delicious! How about yours?"

"I've sold a few paintings down at Jackson Square and painted an army of faces in full festival war paint!" Suzan says.

"I want you to paint the eyes on my face."

"Stop down, I'll give you the cascading eyes and paint eyes on your eyelids so when your eyes are closed they are open!"

"ALRIGHT!" We high five each other and smile.

"Don't worry about what we do." Suzan glares at Eric.

"Especially when we are smoking this hash." I say.

Eric and Chloe plop down next to us around the coffee table. The table looks like it was thrown in a giant washer with every color of the spectrum splattered and dripping all over it.

"It looks like a twisted tornado of color exploded onto your walls." Chloe says.

"I'll take that as a compliment. Are you an artist?" Eric asks Chloe.

"You could say that, I'm a photographer and I write short stories about stories. My philosophy is a simple... Live it, write it and photo it." Chloe says.

"Where's your camera?"

"I'm storing all this on my hard drive! No, I really wish that I had it, I'm on a reckless streak!" Chloe says.

"A reckless adventure is where true art comes from." Chloe says.

"Yes it is a true art that we pursue. The art of debauchery." I say.

"To maintain and not lose the life style is the art. There is a razor edge between the ambient glow of debauchery and the void of destruction."

"So what is everyone doing tonight?" I ask.

"Suzan and I have a costume ball." Eric says.

"I'm up for mad adventure." Chloe says.

"I may have to disappear for the night." I say looking into Chloe's eyes.

"What does that mean?" She asks.

"I've got an appointment with the Louisiana Mojo Man. I've got to pick up my new suit. New Orleans is the only place in America where you can say that you have to pick up a suit and it means a costume." I say.

"Sounds interesting." Suzan says.

"You'll love this one, it is going to be memorable!"

"Tell us your big secret Jas." Chloe says.

"You can come with me and see it first hand."

"I think we're all going to the Howlen' Wolf."

"Yeah you don't want to come, as a matter of fact it is far to dangerous for a cute city girl like yourself." I tell Chloe to get her fired up.

"Says you! I'm coming with you to the Bayou!"

"This girl is spunky." Suzan says.

A solid hour passes by with wonderful abstract artist talk. The pills loosen my jawbone and make the atmosphere warm and conductive. Once we wander back to our agenda Chloe and I decide to get back on the street and get back to our friends in the grip of Salvia high to see if any have lost their minds. After Suzan and I make plans to meet on Jackson Square me and my Mardi Gras Queen are off like a micro parade spilling back onto the dizzy New Orleans streets.

I have bones made out of piano keys and a fusion of melody pours through me into the world as my bones rattle along. The streets are happy with voices and glowing faces that are moven and shaking this Narlins day up like a swarm of bees> The swarm is out searching the wind for natures sweet nectar of chaos and make surreal honey-combs.

"So Chloe would you like to go out to the bayou to meet Emmitt and camp under the stars in my arms?"

"I'd love to Jasper."

"That's the sweetest thing I've heard all week."

"Sweeter than our heavenly breath last night?"

"Sex has no words, you can't compare the two because touch is on an entirely different sensory level than speech. My heart is racing life through my veins!"

"We will be out there in the twigh-light zone. No cops, no bars, and no clothes!"

"Only us and the gators!" I say.

"No worries." Chloe gestures.

The streets are a blur of infinite directions. All possibilities waits for you here. You can take it easy along a crazed parade route with coolers full of beer and ladders stacked with families watching the carnival roll by or you can grab the tiger by the tail! Grab the tiger and have your own ring show complete with fire breathers, wild eyed college kids, freaks, and your more defined 20's and 30's crowd who know how to make Mardi Gras really dangerous and legendary.

Mardi Gras is like being blasted from a circus cannon through a sky full of every high known to the civilized world. Break the chains of reality my friend. Break the mold of conformity, take the trip, I'll see you at the crossroads where we will share a moment of supreme enlightened bliss and push one another all the way! Where, to the crossroads…

Crossroads, crossroads everyone goes down to the deep dark place where the spirits meet. When you hear that call and stumble upon the moon lit night with no street lights and the horizon fades into oblivion. A dusty intersection changes your life, this is what the crossroads are like. See you down in the shifting world of the crossroads . We all will go to the dusty crossroads...

Outside of Ron's I see with a sigh of relief that Moss's truck is still here. I'm curious to hear about the twisted visions they've experienced on the salvia trip.

"The beer is gone." I say.

"Everybody is getting loaded up there."

We look up and everybody is hanging over the balcony with beads and beers in their hands. Chloe throws her shirt up showing her round full breasts with hard nipples that look like they could melt ice. I spin around and moon them! Laughter and moans erupt from the balcony and one of them howls. Beads start to hit the street. I grab a multi colored disco ball necklace and slide it around Chloe's neck, then I wrap my mouth around her left nipple and run the tips of my fingers up her torso, goose bumps cover her skin. This is my language that speaks without words. Chloe is turned on like a plasma blast of white light and I'm blinded by the nebula of her erotic fire.

"You're going to be hard to beat." I say.

"You sure know how to appreciate me, I'm sticking around with you darling."

"That's where you belong!" I laugh.

"You sluts get up here." Andrea yells.

"Coming dear."

"What freaks!" I say as Chloe and I run up the steps to unveil our plan and tell them the unthinkable; that we are leaving. We breaking away from Narlins' for the night. Cheers greet us as we walk through the door, like they missed the hell out of us or something.

"Hello wingnuts!!!" Chloe purrs and her girlfriends scoop her into their arms.

"How did you guys do with the dummy dust?" I ask.

"We broke out the video recorder after you left and captured a special moment." Ron's face turns red and he interjects "Salvia is a very sensual experience. Andrea is teasing him and mimicking his words.

"AH Don't even say it." Ron growls.

"That's bullshit, what are happened?" Chloe asks.

"Alright you're going to find out anyhow."

"Salvia like Ron told you has a feminine presence and while we videoed Ron he got an erection."

"He got a hard on?"

"Hard on? That is not all he got, he came in his pants. We could see a wet spot cream his shorts."

We laugh hysterically but Ron is not embarrassed at all. Instead he is explaining the erotic Salvia Goddess as an exotic mysterious women of sensual pleasure while none of us listen. Maybe the bastard is lucky to have had such a good vision. Terry lights a big joint and I am hydronating with a cold beer. Life is good.

"I'm taking Chloe camping tonight. Anyone care to join us for a night on the Bayou?"

"You're what? I don't think so, we have plans." Andrea objects.

"Yes he is and Ya'll are welcome to join us on the outbound train if anyone of you wants to come along I have an extra boarding pass." Chloe says.

"Hell no, I'm staying right here." Terry says.

"Me too Jasper, tonight is Mardi-Gras and I'm not leaving for nothing." Moss says.

"I've got a special token for you, an admission into the other side of perception to really make the stars come alive." Ron says.

"What do you have Mad Scientist?" I ask.

"A batch of twenty year old DMT stored in a barrel out in the California mountains for the last twenty years, and broke out for Mardi Gras."

"Hot damn, I've always wanted to try DMT."

"Looks like tonight is your night player." Ron says as he hands me a chunk of what looks like a gumball of solid amber crystal. I can see the years of mystery in the luster of this crystal that radiates from under the layer of dust. This looks like red rock incense but Ron assures me this was made way before that scam came into existence. I never like red rock, no offense if you did, but the buzz was missing and I always felt cheated when I smoked the stuff.

Chloe grabs it and after examining it with curious eyes she tells Ron, "thanks love" and slips it into her wooden trinket box with a slide top that has a fairy carved into it.

We wrap up our visit at Ron's because we want to watch the sun set over the Bayou and don't have time to be consumed by the endless highs in Ron's cramped up place. Moss drives Chloe and me to my cave of chaos. I can see a lifelong friend in Chloe. She is as easy to get along with as a summer breeze.

Moss drops us off in front of my place and the fountain greets us behind the gate back to this amazingly tranquil zone. We slam beer and food into the cooler, stuff a load of blankets into the van, roll some joints and in record time we are leaving New Orleans. Leaving the Big Easy is bitter sweet and the feverish wave of consciousness passes through me like water through a storm drain. We are departing. The reward will be beyond what experiences we will have here in the soup of Carnival.

"We are committed to madness." Chloe says.

"If your going to do something, go big. I believe in taking an idea all the way. Once you reach the limit catch your breath and go further."

"I'm loving life with you Jasper."

"Teach me all you know, show me all the secrets of your soul."

"You're an unstoppable rebel, fly me away on your dreamy soul."

"This world was built on dreams Chloe, imagine what kind of a world it would be if it wasn't" I say looking into Chloe's eyes.

"That is beautiful, what made you say that."

"One day I looked into my Grandma's eyes and told her that in her frail state before she moved on. She told me 'You're a dreamer' and I told her that the best things in this world are created from dreams. I looked into her eyes and said, imagine what kind of world this would be if it wasn't."

"What an experience with someone you love so much. It is great you had that connection."

We are leaving the range of New Orleans radio station WWOZ. We drift out of the city and into the swamp as we talk away the miles. Chloe fumbles through the stations and finds static, more and more static, so we throw in a CD my sister sent me from El Salvador, Manu Chao's to transition us into this static.

The weather is warm and my van is getting the recommended daily amount of asphalt, its fill of road. Chloe's eyes are getting wider with each mile as the sun drops on the horizon. I have that sensation that day light is slipping away and I am in a heightened state. We must have tapped into some gypsy voodoo man transmitting energy because I am flying! I've got a talking high that has my head light and dizzy. The sunsets colors unfold before us and we chatter on...

"I read once that when your driving it frees up your mind from all surroundings and sets your mind free. The creative side takes control." I say.

"Yeah that makes sense because nothing has a hold on you, look at those clouds."

"Did you hear anything I just said?"

"Yeah the right, left side of the brain, makes sense." Chloe answers.

"Do this." I bring my hands together, interlocking my fingers with one thumb resting on top of the other while I steer the van with my knee. Chloe does it and as her hands smack together I tell her "Stop, hold them right there. See your left thumb is resting on top of your right thumb."

"Yeah." Chloe looks at her hands then at me.

"Your mind works more from the right side..."

You have finished part one of "The Art of Debauchery." In part two THE ART is realized as we ascend through a journey of conscious chaos in The Art of Debauchery!

VISIT

WWW.ARTOFDEBAUCHERY.COM

POST ANY COMMENTS OR EXPERIENCES

YOU WOULD LIKE TO Share...

also I am launching this platform too...

MUSIC FESTIVAL JUNKIE

www.musicfestivaljunkie.com

Go look at the moon... I got about 20 minutes off and I have to say it is one of the neatest full moons I have ever seen! It looks like a mercury vapor ball glowing with white fire as a pearl would in the shell of a starry sky.

Artwork used with permission by Joe Young, Jason Crawford, Yanni and Drennon...

Catch you all on the flip side!

2-24-2012

Full moon brilliance
when everything is a phantom wisp
The world has become silent
In a moment of clarity
A couple sheets of _ _ is the
American dream still out there?
With my forehead propped against
The inside of the steering wheel
And my eyeballs bouncing off the
dash I would adventure to say
It does exist under these Aboriginal
polka dot sky... The full moon is
Shrouded in angel wings
Cars Roll by with their Ancient
Wisdom on their Bumpers
In a Moment of clarity
Reveals Everything that
Should be Known
The Dream is Alive & it
Is No longer American
It is of the Soul

372

www.ingramcontent.com/pod-product-compliance
Lightning Source LLC
Chambersburg PA
CBHW031100030726
47496CB00002BA/312